MW00809425

DEUTSCHLAND

to P.G.

Richard stopped abruptly a few yards from the red post box, and contemplated its expressionless mouth. He hadn't questioned his decision since he had made it; only now, as it was about to become irreversible, did these last few yards feel difficult. He looked around furtively. No one was watching.

The letter he had written the night before was still in the inside pocket of his grey jacket. He had spent hours making sure that the form he had downloaded from the Internet at the public library was filled in clearly, that the right payment details had been given, and that nothing had been overlooked.

After careful consideration he had decided to omit his phone number in the box provided, choosing to write 'No phone' instead. He was somewhat confident it had been the right thing to do, for what if there were an error and someone from the university had to telephone him? If, as was likely, the telephone were not answered by him he might need to explain himself before he was ready.

When he had received Robert's message he'd known that the time had come. He was feeling his age and thought he owed it to himself and those he loved to revisit this part of his past. And he had timed it smartly. This summer the house would be full of children and the distractions they inevitably brought. Distraction for his family to give him the privacy to look into what he had done, as well as distractions for him as he was waiting for the test results.

Pulled back to the present, Richard wondered how long he had been standing there. Even in this quiet part of the village, it wouldn't be long before he attracted attention. He reached for his inside pocket, and was briefly flustered when he couldn't immediately feel the envelope. But then he managed to locate it, and walked the last few steps towards the post box, finally fitting the description of a man about to post a letter.

He was aware that only once he had pushed the letter through the slot would he know how he really felt about having completed this step. But maybe even then it wouldn't be too late. He could wait for the post van to pull up and then plead with its driver to have the letter returned. Would the postman take his word that it was his, or was there a code postmen had to follow that would not allow them to return letters once they had been posted, no matter how insistent the senders, no matter how convincing the arguments?

Richard hesitated for only the briefest of moments before he pushed the letter through the slot and it dropped into the post box. As he heard the envelope come to rest, he was surprised that he felt nothing.

1

Her right forearm still hurt from the last time they had been there. It was a lingering pain – more a reminder of what he had made her do than a part of the healing process. She had read all about pain yesterday, when they were hanging out in Granddad's study and the others had gone to fetch some supplies – crisps and Coke, and some slices of apples, which they'd ignored until they turned brown and could be discarded. Pain, Sam had read, was not the side effect of an injury, but there to help the body take care of itself, a warning sign for its owner to pay attention and give it a chance to heal. But she *knew* she was hurt, and she *knew* that it was all Tony's fault, so what was the point of being warned?

'I'm bored,' Tony announced from the armchair, almost disappearing into its cushions. As usual, Sam was sitting on the windowsill, her left shoulder pressed against the cold glass. The rain had kept them in for most of the summer holidays so far, and Sam and her brothers were once again stuck in the front lounge of their grandparents' house. This was far less entertaining than Granddad's study, one floor above, but that was off limits when he took his afternoon nap. At least from up there they could make out the sea in the distance if the weather was good enough. Down here all they could see was the driveway, and not much else. Even when the sun was out, it was the darkest room in the house – an overhanging willow tree that should have been cut back aeons ago saw to that.

They regarded the lounge as more of a waiting room, a place to wait for something to happen, than a useful place to be. It was where their grandma kept most of her precious things – framed photographs of Mum and her sister, Kate, bold-coloured vases made by local craftsmen, and a collection of old-fashioned records of sad music, which Sam wouldn't admit in a million years she liked – making it nigh on impossible to move without risking breaking something, at least if you were under ten, stuck indoors and itching to be occupied.

'I am bored, too,' Jeff said. Sam's younger brother was sitting on the striped carpet by the fireplace, which looked as if it hadn't been used in years. He was playing with the set of marbles he had won the previous weekend at the fair in the nearby town. He was using a couple of wine corks as goalposts and had divided his marbles into two teams, which now seemed to be in the middle of a penalty shoot-out. He didn't look bored at all, as far as Sam could see.

'We could read something,' she suggested.

'Reading is *boring*,' Tony said, contempt in his voice.

Yesterday Sam, Tony and Jeff had been reading all day. Well, Sam was doing most of the reading, while Tony and Jeff were looking at the pictures. Tony would only read out the captions to pictures he took a particular interest in, invariably those to do with torture and death. There were tons of books to be found in Granddad's study – some for kids, but some definitely *not* for kids – and with the endless rain, they had gone through practically the whole library. They had discovered a book about Egyptians and how they buried their dead. They even buried their cats with full ceremony.

Sam rolled down her sleeve over her singed forearm. She should have disappeared to do some drawing, but with Grandma doing her painting so well Sam found it hard to get the inspiration. She wished she was good at something, like Grandma was at painting or Mum was at jewellery design or Dad at writing, but she easily got frustrated when she tried something and failed. And with their parents away during the week, she took it upon herself to keep her two brothers out of trouble, and that was a chore enough. She dare not leave them alone for long.

'I'm bored *to death*,' Tony elaborated, and Sam knew that if she didn't do something to relieve Tony of his boredom there might be trouble again. He'd suggest doing something crazy and Sam had two choices: play along and make the best of it, or say she wasn't coming. If she refused to take part it would be, 'Samantha is *sooo* boring, Samantha is such a sissy, Samantha is such a *girl* . . .' all summer long, or what was left of it.

'We could see what Granddad has got in the shed,' Sam suggested. The shed seemed harmless enough.

'Nothing interesting in there. I had a look yesterday,' Tony said. He had started to emerge from the cushions and Sam knew that he was dying to suggest something to do.

'When yesterday?' she asked.

'Day before yesterday, then. I didn't see anything.'

'There must be something,' Sam said half-heartedly.

'What about the beach?' It was Jeff who suggested it. He didn't know any better.

Tony smiled.

'It's raining cats and dogs,' Sam said, and Jeff giggled.

'It stopped *pissing down* ages ago,' Tony said. He got up lazily from the armchair, walked over to Sam and looked through the window. It was still raining a little, but to her disappointment Sam saw a patch of blue sky in the distance and it looked like it was headed their way. They'd have to go out and play one of Tony's games.

'I don't want to do that again,' Sam said.

'Come on, let's go,' Tony said. 'Or are you chicken or what?' He unconsciously pulled his fingers through his short black hair so that it stuck up in aggressive spikes.

Sam reluctantly got up from the windowsill.

'Chicken!' Jeff repeated. She looked at him furiously. He was only five, and she supposed that she should forgive him, but for a moment she was in two minds about trying to protect him from Tony's stupid games. If she didn't, though, who would?

While the boys fetched the bikes from the shed, Sam went to tell Grandma that they were going to the beach. By the time Sam stepped outside the house, Tony was already on his bike. Jeff patiently waited for Sam to tie his shoelaces, so that he could get on his.

The forest that separated their part of the village from the sea started right behind Sam's grandparents' house. From the window of Granddad's study you could see that the sea was no further than half a mile away, but once you were in the middle of the forest, often not sure of which way to turn, it could feel miles away.

Sam and Jeff grabbed their bikes, which were leaning against the side of the house, and followed Tony through the large back garden. In Sam's opinion the garden was rather wasted on her grandparents, although they had made some half-hearted attempts at getting it into shape over the years. But Grandma and Granddad weren't outdoorsy people and used it only to sit out in summer to read their newspapers and books.

The children walked past the overgrown pond, where a lone yellow plastic duck had floated for as long as anyone could remember, and opened the small green wire-meshed gate at the back of the garden. They had to squeeze themselves and their bikes through a collection of bushes to reach the footpath, which was layered in places with paving stones but mostly had been formed by generations of visitors to the forest compacting the earth. Years ago this path might have been distinct enough to offer an enticing route past the village, but with ramblers rare these days it had become increasingly overgrown.

It was still drizzling a little, but despite her misgivings Sam felt good getting out into the fresh air after being stuck indoors. A neighbour had mown his grass and, after the rain, it smelled delicious. She took a deep breath. The scent of grass mixed with the salt from the sea: the smell of summer holidays.

As usual, Tony was cycling in front, Sam a close second, with Jeff left trailing behind. Sam took an occasional peek back at Jeff to make sure they hadn't lost him. Even little Jeff was a bit oversized for the bike he was riding. They had been given the bikes two summers ago and now they were all just a bit too small.

The path, uneven with tree roots, muddy or soft with beech mast, took seemingly unending twists and turns, and frequently decisions would have to be made about which to take, but it had been a while since the children had got lost. As the path wound through the dense forest, the uninitiated would have almost given up hope, but even Jeff knew that if you stuck at it, almost by magic, you turned a corner and there it was. Their secret beach.

As usual it was deserted. They got off their bikes and laid them down at the edge of the forest.

Their beach had a little of everything: rocks that led right up to the shoreline, which fifty yards or so further down gave way to beautiful sand. That part wouldn't have been out of place in a holiday brochure, albeit without the sun. The rain had now cleared, and the sun was struggling to come out, but the wind was cold and strong enough to make the beach an unpleasant place to be.

Tony had gone ahead. 'I bet I can beat you again,' he turned and shouted once Sam and Jeff were in earshot before continuing briskly towards the edge of the sea.

'Not if you play fair,' Sam said.

'What do you mean?' Tony looked back for a second at Sam. 'I play fair.'

'*Of course* you do.' Sam didn't know why, but she felt like needling him, even though it would probably only make things worse.

'You asking for trouble?' Tony clenched his fist.

'No,' she said quietly. She thought that Tony wouldn't be able to beat her up even if he tried, but she wasn't yet ready to rob him of his illusion. He may have been almost two years older, but he was not that much taller than Sam. 'May the best person win,' she said a little louder into the wind, and with as much sarcasm as she could muster. She had only recently got the hang of sarcasm and was enjoying it.

Tony stopped at an abandoned little wooden boat, not much longer than six foot, which rested upside down right at the edge of the sea. There was a big hole in the front, and Sam couldn't help wondering about the person who had carefully painted it dark blue and given it a wildly optimistic name – *Discovery*. Whoever washed up here couldn't have been too happy, she thought. At least now it had been given a new lease of life, at any rate for this summer, when Tony had decided to appropriate it for hiding stuff they either couldn't be bothered to take all the way back to the house, or about which questions would be asked.

Tony got on his knees and reached into the hole of the boat. Quickly he retrieved the dented old oil canister they had found. You could find pretty much anything around this little stretch of coast if you looked long enough.

He stood up, canister in hand, and licked his index finger. He held it up in the air to determine where the wind came from, even though it was pretty obvious to Sam, whose long brown hair seemed to act like one of those windsocks they had at airports, and she frequently had to brush it out of her face. Sam wished they had gone away on holiday somewhere warm and sunny with their parents, but things were just too busy at work, as had been announced at the kitchen table one dinnertime.

Tony walked over to the back of the boat, which, even though only two foot high, provided some essential shelter from the wind. He placed the canister in the centre of the makeshift fireplace, fashioned from stones, next to some slim branches and twigs they had collected a few days ago from the forest. Other bits of kindling had scattered a few feet from where they had placed them. Sam picked up some twigs.

'They're damp,' she observed, trying to hide her relief. 'Got to do this some other time.'

Instead of an answer, Tony went back to the open side of the boat and retrieved some spare branches he had stashed away. He looked at Sam defiantly. Sam cursed herself that he had thought of it. Tony didn't usually plan that far ahead. As a final tease he produced a newspaper from the back pocket of his jeans.

'What's that?' Sam asked.

'A newspaper, stupid.'

'I meant, where did you get it?' Sam was pretty sure it was today's; she recognised the headline. The grown-ups had been talking about it at lunch. Something about a war.

'It's Granddad's. He doesn't need it any more.'

'How do you know?'

'I asked.'

Sam bet he hadn't, even though Granddad would no doubt have given it to him, but she couldn't be bothered to argue. Now they were here, they might as well get it over with. She had told Grandma they would be back in good time for dinner. *Dead or alive*, she had been tempted to add. Contemplating Tony, Sam thought that Grandma was far too trusting. If I ever have kids, I'll keep an eye on them night and day, she decided.

Tony tore off a couple of sheets of the newspaper and crumpled it up. He put it in the canister and added a few branches. He reached under the boat again and retrieved a bottle of white spirit they had borrowed from the shed at the beginning of the holiday. They could tell from the mildewed label it must have been there for years so would hardly be missed. Anyway, Granddad's memory wasn't as it used to be, Sam thought. Last week, he had been looking for one of his books all day, only for Grandma to point out that she had seen him take it back to the library the day before. The kids had found it dead funny, but Granddad, who rarely minded being the butt of a joke, seemed to take it the wrong way and was quiet all evening. He'd been unusually quiet this holiday, Sam thought.

Tony opened the bottle and poured some of the clear liquid over the wood, almost as if he were dressing a salad. He handed the bottle and top to Sam. She screwed on the top and placed the bottle back in the hole of the boat.

'Matches,' Tony said. Sam had already retrieved them

from the hiding place, and handed him the box. Tony had procured the matches at the beginning of the holidays. Sam didn't ask him where from, not least because she knew he was longing to tell her. He took a match out of the box, and struck it. It didn't light on the first attempt, and Sam hoped that they might all have got damp, but on the second attempt it sparked happily into life.

Tony threw it on to the twigs. The fire immediately flared out far from the canister, and the children all instinctively took a couple of steps back until the flames receded.

'It's my go first,' Tony said. Sam knew why. The fire looked hotter now, but when the wood started to glow red-hot, it would be hot as hell. When it was *her* turn.

Tony stood closer to the canister and put his hand over the flame, high enough for it not to start burning immediately but low enough that it would start to in a few seconds, and then hurt like hell a few seconds later.

'One, two . . .' Tony counted.

A couple of days ago Tony had lasted a whole eight seconds, and Sam only half that, but even those four seconds were long enough for her arm still to be hurting now. She decided that today she would use her other arm. At first Tony hadn't allowed Jeff to have a go, but Sam knew that he would tease him mercilessly for not taking part later. She had helped find a small crate, one of those used for vegetables at the market. It wouldn't have been fair if his arm had been closer to the fire because he was shorter. The crate was just strong enough for Jeff to stand on and have his go, even if only for a couple of seconds.

'. . . three, four, five . . .' It was hard to tell if Tony was hurting or not, but he wasn't looking at them any more.

Sam felt her smarting arm. She knew she didn't really have to do this, but if she won today, Tony would forget about the game. He would probably think of another one, but until he did, they'd have some breathing space.

'. . . six, seven . . .' The gaps between the counting were definitely getting shorter, but Sam didn't want to complain. It didn't look like Tony could last much longer. Sam hoped he wasn't doing himself any serious harm.

'. . . eight, nine!' Tony withdrew his hand as quickly as he could and Sam thought she could see tears welling up in his eyes. He turned away.

'A new world record! I won!' he announced when the pain didn't show on his face any more.

'Not so fast,' Sam said, and rolled up the left sleeve of her shirt as far as it would go. 'I haven't had my turn yet.'

'What? You think you can turn *four seconds* into a new world record?' Tony said. Jeff looked up at him, and Sam knew that Jeff would have a go if Tony wanted him to. 'It's your turn, Jeff,' Tony said. Jeff looked pleased.

'No, he's too young,' Sam said.

'Bullshit he's too young,' Tony said. 'He did it last time, didn't he? Even if it was only one second.' Tony looked at Jeff with barely disguised contempt.

'Let me go first!' Sam said, but Jeff was already beginning to roll up his shirt. It got stuck halfway. Sam found herself helping him. At least he wouldn't burn his shirt – that would take some explaining.

'Ready?' Tony asked.

Sam grabbed the crate and put it next to the canister for Jeff to stand on.

Tony looked on impatiently. 'Hurry up!'

'We're ready,' Sam confirmed, but with Jeff's weight the crate had already sunk a little into the ground, and it didn't look high enough.

Jeff put his small hand over the fire. Sam could see that he was closer to the fire than Tony had been.

'One . . .' Tony counted.

'That's not fair,' Sam said. 'He's too close.' She could see Jeff biting his lip.

'Two . . .'

Sam knew she would have to do something. Jeff was in pain. He was burning, and he was her responsibility.

'Three . . .' Tony looked at Sam. Sam tore herself from his gaze and pushed Jeff away from the flames.

'Hey! What did you do that for?' Jeff complained.

'You were burning up!' Sam shouted.

'I was not!'

'You were, too,' Sam said. 'Let's have a look.' Jeff reluctantly offered his forearm for examination. It was singed. Some of the fine hair had turned black. Sam couldn't help but touch it.

'Ouch!'

'You're such a chicken,' Tony said, but only half-heartedly. He too had taken a peek at Jeff's arm over Sam's shoulders. If their parents found out they'd be grounded for life.

'He's not a chicken,' Sam mumbled under her breath. 'He did it, didn't he?' She gave Tony a look that could kill.

'Let's get out of here,' Tony said.

'Not so fast,' Sam said. 'It's my go.' Tony may have started this, but she would finish it – for her sake, and for Jeff's.

'You won't beat me,' Tony said. 'I said let's get out of here.'

Instead of a reply, Sam stepped up next to the canister and put her left arm above the fire, the same height at which Tony had placed his. She could see that the fire was red-hot by now. Immediately the flames started to bite.

'One, two . . .' Sam counted. She was half afraid that Tony and Jeff would leave her on her own and was relieved when she heard Tony complaining nearby, 'You're counting too fast!'

'. . . three . . . four . . .' Sam counted a little slower and closed her eyes. She could feel the heat on her face.

'You'll never make it.'

'. . . five . . .' She bit her lip. She had broken her own record, but to break Tony's record still seemed impossible. Another five long seconds to go and only then would she have made it.

'. . . six . . . seven . . .' Sam's arm had really started to burn, but she fought the instinct to pull it away from the heat. If she gave up now Tony would laugh at her and Jeff would follow, and they would probably have to do the challenge all over again in a couple of days. Tony never got tired of games he won.

'. . . eight . . . nine . . .' If Sam's eyes had been open, she would have seen Tony moving away, losing interest.

'. . . ten . . .'

'Hey, you've done it!' Jeff shouted, but Sam didn't hear. 'Stop!'

'. . . eleven . . .'

Jeff grabbed her by her shirt and pulled her away from the fire, and she almost fell on the ground. She felt immense relief at first, but then suddenly her arm was stinging intensely. Jeff had tears in his eyes. Sam didn't know how much longer she would have lasted and she was glad that Jeff had grabbed her. Once she had crossed the pain threshold, she had felt as if she could keep her arm there for ever.

Somehow she managed to compose herself, despite the pain of her blistered skin, and when Tony had turned away, she winked at Jeff.

'I'm bored, come on!' Tony said, already halfway to where they had left their bikes. His record broken, he seemed in a hurry to get home.

'What about the fire?'

'It can burn itself out,' Tony shouted. 'Or are you afraid the sea will catch fire?'

Sam managed a half-smile. She looked down at her singed forearm. The blisters would take ages to heal, but even though her arm hurt like hell, her pride was intact. More than intact: she had won. She started to make her way slowly towards the bikes too.

'Wait for me!' Jeff was having problems with his shoelaces again, and Sam stopped to tie them. He should have learned how to do it by now, she thought, but maybe he liked the attention.

'I'm really sorry for yelling at you,' she said quietly when she had finished, and Jeff had got on his feet again.

'That's OK.'

'Thank you.' Sam gave Jeff a hug, but quickly let go when her hurting arm touched his back.

Tony had already disappeared into the forest. Sam let Jeff cycle in front of her so she could keep an eye on him. She was the last to get on her bike, and as she took one final glance back at the sea she shivered.

2

When he heard the rattle of the letterbox Richard sat up quietly, and his feet reached for the brown slippers waiting at his side of the bed. Every morning since he had posted the letter he would wake as soon as it became light. Lying in bed, listening to Suzannah breathing quietly beside him, he listened out impatiently, calculating in his mind how long it might take for the package to reach him.

He stood up and quietly put on his dressing gown, draped over the armchair beside where he stood. He had started placing it there, instead of on the hook of the door of the en-suite bathroom. If Suzannah had noticed it, she certainly hadn't found it unusual enough to make a comment. As he crossed the room, Richard was careful to avoid the floorboards he knew might creak. He opened the door without making a sound, and closed it behind him.

As Richard stole past the boys' room, its door left ajar to catch some of the light from the hallway, he couldn't resist taking a glance inside, if only to make sure that they were still asleep. They seemed pretty much in the same positions in which he had put them to bed last night. They had been exhausted, as was he. It was a pleasure to have the children for the summer and, despite the commotion and disruption in his routine their long stays inevitably caused, he was always sad when it was time for them to go.

As Richard turned, his left foot inadvertently kicked a marble and he looked on helplessly as it rolled silently on the thick carpet towards the stairs. For a moment it appeared as if it might come to rest before the end of the landing, but then it dropped off the edge of the carpet and descended the stairs, hitting each of the wooden steps with the ear-splitting reverberation that is possible only when a house is quiet. After many painful seconds it mercifully came to a halt somewhere in the corridor below.

Richard, stopped in his tracks, waited to see if it had woken anyone. After listening to the silence for a few moments, he continued his journey downstairs.

The grand staircase was one of the main reasons Suzannah had bought the house with her first husband, and, not for the first time, Richard felt a little small descending it. He had lived in this old house long enough to know it inside out, delighting in watching it grow even older with him, sometimes resisting, as best as he could, the minor repairs Suzannah would suggest. But while the house could be fixed almost definitively, he knew he could not.

He had watched three generations grow up: his own, the one of the children he had never had (friends' children, observed at a safe distance) and now Suzannah's children's children. He felt uncomfortable calling them his grandchildren. Even after fifteen years, his new family still felt borrowed to him. Who could say for certain that a third man would not step into his shoes once he had gone?

When he reached the ground floor he walked briskly along the long corridor to the small entrance hall, the morning light glowing through the antique glass front door, reflecting all the colours of the rainbow on the walls.

Today's mail lay in a pile on the chequered tiled floor. At first glance it looked like the usual mix of bills, one or two thick catalogues and junk mail, but Richard needed to make sure. With some effort, resting on his left knee, he leaned down to pick up the pile of mail, but stopped short when he heard footsteps approaching on the gravel outside the house.

Instinctively, he ducked to the side of the door. Through the stained-glass side panel he could make out the outline of someone approaching. The person walked up the path determinedly, and Richard drew back further. He was waiting for the doorbell to ring, blowing his cover. Instead, the letterbox opened and the weekly local newspaper dropped through, and joined the pile of mail on the floor. He let out a sigh of relief when he heard the footsteps retreat.

Slightly flustered, Richard picked up the mail and stood up. He flicked through it. When he couldn't find what he was looking for he carefully held the pile of mail at the same height as the letterbox and dropped it back on to the floor to give the impression that it had not been disturbed.

Satisfied with the freshly re-formed pile, the local paper placed on top as his *pièce de résistance*, he entered the kitchen. The kitchen table was already set for breakfast, prepared by Suzannah the evening before to allow everyone to follow his or her own schedule. First the children, then Suzannah, then her daughter Kate, who was staying with them for a little while, would drift out of bed. Only at the weekend, when the children's parents came to stay, would everyone be at breakfast at the same time.

For Richard the pleasures of a family breakfast would never fade. An only child, he'd had his breakfast prepared for him by his mother, who stood next to him while he ate it, smoking her first of many cigarettes, until he was ready to be packed off on the school bus. His father had usually left for work long before Richard got up, if he was at home at all. By the time Richard had become a teenager his father's absences were the rule rather than the exception.

Richard took a glass from the cupboard. He remembered his father taking him to the occasional baseball game, of course, but when he tried to picture him it was just that: a faint black-and-white picture of a man in a chipped golden frame on a mantelpiece, holding his son's hand. Richard was looking up at him laughing, his father mischievously gazing in the direction of the photographer. The joke they had shared was long forgotten, and where the photo was taken Richard could not remember. He had detested his father for his absences until much later in life it occurred to him that he had little choice in so far as the raising of his son was concerned: he could either be a friend to him or put clothes on his back.

Richard turned on the tap, let it run until the water felt cool and fresh to his finger, and filled his glass. He sat down on his chair. His place at the table was in a slightly awkward position so that he would have to move his chair every time one of the children wanted to get up and fetch something – but this was the seat he'd chosen when he moved in here, taking the place, but not the seat, of another man. Coincidence, perhaps, but the seat Richard had chosen was the only one from where the wall of family pictures could not be seen.

One day Richard surprised Suzannah in the process of removing the picture of her first husband sitting at this very table. Richard was quick to insist that removing the photo would not be necessary. He knew that they had different lives, he insisted, and he knew that Suzannah's life had been rich in experiences and lovers and his had not. After the first months and years had passed, and Richard kept seeing the picture on the wall, he had wished that he had accepted Suzannah's offer to remove it, but now it was too late. He had started to resent her for listening to him, for not reading between the lines, even though he always insisted that with him what you saw was what you got.

The chair that used to be occupied by Suzannah's former husband was now occupied by Kate whenever she was staying, and remained empty when she wasn't: those long spells when they hardly ever heard from her, until the phone rang to announce her imminent arrival, often from a London train station. Whenever Richard happened to pick up the receiver and heard railway announcements in the background, he knew before she had even said a word that Kate was coming home, that some upset in her life had caused her to seek them, or that she had good news that was worth sharing.

For Richard, home had been New York City, but leaving had been much easier than he had thought. He had instantly fallen for an English woman, a gregarious, beautiful woman who was way out of his league. They had met at a conference – in New York, of course, as he hardly ever went anywhere else. They were queuing up for the buffet dinner, she right behind him. He turned, saw her and never turned back.

The two strangers sat together at a quiet table in the corner of the former ballroom and Richard found it easy to talk to her, or at least listen to her, with her sharp wit, quickly disseminating her fellow biologists and dividing the speakers into separate groups for dullness and errors in their expertise. He would have enjoyed her observations even more if he had actually been a participant of the conference, but he took too much pleasure in Suzannah's company to reveal the actual reason for his presence, fearing that she might lose all interest in him. He had been sent to supervise the repair of the air-conditioning system, and was rewarded with a free dinner in return for the efficiency of his small team. For most of the evening he answered Suzannah's questions vaguely enough to fit in with whatever scenario she had pictured for him without having to tell an outright lie. He had wanted to make sure that she had also fallen in love with him before she became aware of the mundanity of his existence.

After dinner, she decided to skip the invitation to a formal function organised by the conference. She and Richard stayed until they were the last two left in the hotel restaurant, then moved to the bar, and when that closed too and there was no place else to go, Suzannah invited him up to her room. Richard never quite knew at what point of the evening Suzannah realised that he was not a fellow participant, and if she had ever been disappointed, she didn't show it.

Soon there was no question about whether they should live together or not; the only question was who would compromise for whom. The old country or the new? They settled for the old, or rather it just happened that way. A few weeks after the conference, fearing that their love might not last across continents, Richard went on his first trip to England and never returned – not because he loved the old country that much; it just seemed easier for him to sever his connections in the US than for Suzannah to sever hers in England. His job was easy to give up, and had never given him much satisfaction.

The night before he was due to take his flight back home, he called a friend on a crackly transatlantic phone line and asked him to pack up his things and help dissolve the two-room apartment in Queens he had occupied for half his life. He never saw his friend again.

Richard didn't know how long he had been sitting in the kitchen, but he noticed that the glass he had been drinking from was now empty. The children would be up soon. He walked over to the sink, where he filled the glass once more, as an alibi in case Suzannah had woken in his absence. Glass in hand, he left the kitchen and made his way back towards the stairs.

He was pleased with himself when he remembered the marble. Searching for it took some effort, and he was conscious of the time, but eventually he spotted it behind the base of the coat stand. He kneeled down to retrieve it, for a moment uncertain of what to do with his glass, and then decided to put it on the radiator. He picked up the marble, and, once he had climbed the stairs, replaced it precisely where he had disturbed it.

3

'Whoever makes it to the beach and back first is the undisputed winner,' Tony explained, restlessly sitting on his bike behind the garden gate at the edge of the forest. 'You've got to pick up a stone to prove you were there.'

Sam suspected that Tony was up to one of his old tricks. She took a deep breath of fresh air, feeling more confident since she had beaten him the day before. She decided that she wouldn't let him win just to keep trouble at bay. As far as Tony's challenges went, racing was pretty harmless. Anyway, even if he got tired of it and they ended up hanging out at the beach, the stupid challenge with the fire was over and done with now.

'Three, two, one . . . Jeff go!'

As usual Jeff got a head start. Not enough to make a real difference, but even Tony agreed it was only fair to give his brother a couple of seconds' lead.

'Three, two, one . . . go!'

Almost immediately Tony overtook Jeff, then took an unexpected turn, which Sam was sure would lead him in the wrong direction, but who cared? Jeff raced after Tony, and Sam decided to stick with her brothers. She was also about to overtake Jeff when she noticed that his shoelaces had become untied again.

'Jeff, careful!' she shouted, but it was too late. One shoelace had caught in the chain of his bike. Sam watched Jeff come off, almost in slow motion.

'Shit!' Sam stopped so quickly she almost fell herself. Jeff was lying on the ground a few yards behind her.

'Tony, wait!' Sam shouted into the forest as she dismounted, but Tony had already gone. She ran over to Jeff, who was holding his knee, and biting his lips. 'Are you OK?'

He nodded, but she could see that he was suppressing his tears.

'Let me see.' Sam leaned down to examine his knee. Jeff let go and she inspected the damage. It was all bloody, but she had seen worse. 'Ouch. That must hurt.'

'Not much,' Jeff said, trying to put on a brave face. 'I'm sorry I made you lose the race.'

'That's OK.'

When she heard Tony behind her she turned. He had returned on his bike, clutching a stone in his left hand – far too soon to be probable – but she decided to ignore it.

'What's up?' Tony asked.

'Jeff came off his bike.'

He looked down at Jeff without getting off. 'Can't you do anything right?'

'Leave him alone,' Sam said, annoyed. 'Can't you see he's hurt?'

'Just a scratch,' Tony announced, and Jeff looked up at him, tears in his eyes. 'What? Are you going to cry, sissy boy?'

'Leave him alone.' Sam took a tissue from her back pocket, spat on it and began to clean up Jeff's knee as best she could.

'Why? What are you going to do?' Tony asked, sneering. 'Are you going to beat me up?' But he made no move to get off his bike.

Sam stood up, and turned to Tony. She was just thinking that he looked a little worried when she became aware of a faint noise. 'What's that?' she asked.

'What's what?' Tony asked, irritated, but unable to hide his curiosity completely.

'That noise.'

'What noise?'

'Shush.' Sam could make out a quiet, steady buzzing sound, almost like a swarm of bees, only too constant for it to be made by anything alive. 'It's coming from somewhere behind there,' she said, pointing at the thick bushes that lined the right side of the path.

'Let's take a look.' Tony finally got off his bike.

Full of trepidation, Sam made her way towards the shrubs. Jeff was on his feet again, distracted from his pain. Before Sam could decide on how to proceed, Tony pushed past them. He crouched and disappeared through a small gap in the bushes.

'Through here,' he shouted from between the bushes. 'I can see something.' Sam, and then Jeff, limping a little, squeezed themselves through the opening Tony had found. Once she had emerged at the other side, Sam had to cover her eyes. Everything seemed much brighter all of a sudden.

'Wow,' Tony said.

The three of them stood in a clearing in the middle of the forest. It was perhaps as large as a public swimming pool; old stumps of trees lined the ground, with some saplings having defied the cull and grown a yard high or so. Sam took a quick glance around: there seemed to be no proper entrance to the clearing. No wonder they hadn't noticed it before, even though they must have passed close by dozens of times.

'What's that?' Jeff asked, pointing towards the centre and the source of the buzzing sound.

'I don't know,' Sam said, although she did have some idea.

A set of two tall wire-mesh fences about a yard apart surrounded an electricity substation. A dilapidated sign on the fence read 'HIGH VOLTAGE – KEEP CLEAR' and next to it another underlined the point with the image of a skull and crossbones.

'It must be some kind of electricity generator,' Sam said. There were two sets of transformers connected with numerous cables to a pylon that reached up into the sky.

'I didn't know this was here,' Tony said. He must be quite upset, Sam thought. The forest was his territory, and he always pretended to know it like the back of his hand. He turned to her. 'Did you?'

'No,' she reassured him.

'Is it dangerous?' Jeff asked.

'I don't suppose,' Sam said. It does *look* dangerous, she thought, but she tried to give her voice some kind of reassuring tone. After all, this thing wasn't about to attack them, even if the buzzing was horribly loud. She wondered why they had never noticed it before. Too busy with other things, she decided.

'Of course it's dangerous,' Tony said, and stepped out into the clearing like a courageous explorer. He was trying to make up for the initial discovery of unexplored territory he had missed out on. No, he liked it here, and she was not going to take it away from him. He'd probably argue that if it hadn't been for him, they would never have come here, so by rights this new and creepy place was his.

'Do you think there's electricity in this?' he asked,

pointing at the fence with the 'HIGH VOLTAGE' sign, but he wasn't really expecting an answer.

'I don't know. I guess so,' Sam said, following cautiously. She realised that she was holding Jeff's hand. The buzzing noise became louder, and she could feel the hairs rising on the back of her neck.

'Only one way of finding out.' Tony stepped close up to the fence and slowly reached out his hands to touch it.

'Don't!' Sam shouted, when his hands were only an inch or so away from the fence.

'I'm not chicken,' Tony said, and gripped the fence with both hands. As soon as he touched it, he started to tremble.

'Tony!' Sam screamed, but even though she wanted to, she didn't dare touch him. She had done a first-aid course at school, and knew better than to touch someone who was being electrocuted. After a few seconds Tony fell back from the fence and on to the ground. He just lay there – his body looked lifeless.

'Are you all right?' Sam ran over and kneeled down next to him. He didn't look OK. She started to shake him, gently at first, then more and more violently, but he didn't move. She feverishly tried to remember what to do from the first-aid lesson, but her mind was a complete blank. 'Say something!' She was close to tears before she began to sense that something was not quite right. Tony was still breathing. She had an idea. She started to tickle him under his arms. In less than a second he was giggling uncontrollably.

'Booo!' Tony said, opening his eyes, but much too late to have the desired effect.

'That's not fair!' Sam shouted, and got up on her feet. 'I thought you were dead!'

'Dead? From that thing? You're such a chicken.'

'You scared me to death!'

Then all three of them heard the snap of an electric spark and they fell quiet. When they heard another spark, Tony got up and brushed the grass off his jeans. He put his hands on the fence again and looked through it at the transformer. Sam and Jeff also stepped closer to take a look, but Sam didn't feel much like touching the fence, electrified or not.

Above the transformer a loose wire leading up to the pylon moved precariously in the light breeze. Whenever it touched the transformer it sparked noisily. Sam looked at Tony and saw that he was as unsettled as she was.

'Let's go home,' she said.

'Yeah. I'm hungry,' Tony said, and let go of the fence.

4

Sam's mum, Francesca, hugged her as tight as she could. Hugs were a serious business in her family – they had to last at least seven seconds, otherwise they were not deemed worth having.

'How much I have missed you all!' Francesca announced to her parents, children and sister, who were already sitting down to dinner. As usual Sam's parents were running late. They were down for a long weekend as a nod to the summer holidays.

'It's only been four and a half days, Mum,' Jeff said from the table, tucking into his macaroni cheese.

'I know, but I still missed you, darling. I'm your mum and mums are allowed to miss their children for four days. Four and *a half* days.' Francesca hugged Jeff. 'Look, I even brought your father.'

'I am sorry, I got stuck in the office . . .' Robert said as he entered the kitchen, and Jeff rushed to give him a hug.

Francesca noticed Jeff's untied shoelaces. 'Have you been walking around like that all day?' Before Jeff returned to his seat, Francesca kneeled down to tie them. She glanced at Sam.

'I've been tying them all holiday,' Sam said, a little annoyed.

When Francesca had finished tying the shoelaces, she noticed the scratch on Jeff's knee. 'What's happened here?'

'Nothing,' Jeff said.

'Did you fall?'

Jeff nodded.

'He just came off his bike,' Tony said. 'Nothing serious.'

'Are you OK?' Francesca looked into Jeff's eyes and took hold of both of his arms to pull him closer. Sam cringed. If the singe on Jeff's forearm was half as bad as hers she knew it wouldn't have healed yet. Sam could see Jeff bite his lip.

'Mmm,' Jeff said.

'It must hurt,' Francesca said.

'A bit,' Jeff said, and Francesca let go of his arm.

'Let's clean it up and I'll get you a plaster.'

Jeff looked at Sam, and Sam winked at him. With his cherubic face, Jeff was accepted by everyone to be his mother's darling.

'So, what have you guys been up to?' Robert asked, as he sat down at the table, taking a steaming plate of pasta from Suzannah.

'Nothing,' Tony said.

'Must've been interesting,' Francesca smiled, having returned with a box of plasters, trying to get the Cellophane wrapper off.

'It was,' Jeff said, and Tony tried to silence him with a glance, but Jeff didn't seem to notice. 'It sparks and everything,' he added.

'What sparks?' Suzannah asked, putting another generous plateful down in Francesca's place.

'We discovered some kind of decrepit electricity thingy in the forest.' Sam tried hard to make it sound as boring as possible. 'Some kind of generator. It must be really old. Doesn't look like much.'

'It's nothing really,' Tony added. 'Behind the bushes on the way to the beach.'

Tony glanced at Sam gratefully. It felt good to be on the same side for once, she thought.

'It's not still being used, is it?' Suzannah asked.

'It sparks and everything,' Jeff said again.

'That's just the wind, stupid,' Tony said, kicking his brother under the table. 'I don't think it's being used. It's nothing really. There are two big fences around it.'

'I don't think we'll go there again,' Sam said, but she knew the battle was lost. 'It really isn't much fun.' She could have recognised her mum's look a mile away, and knew what was coming.

'I want you kids to stay away from it,' Francesca said. 'Whether it's working or not, it's still dangerous.'

Sam and Tony looked at each other and understood, and Jeff would too, once Tony explained to him that rules were made to be broken.

'I really don't think it's still being used,' Tony said.

Francesca ignored him. 'I want you to promise me.'

Tony looked at Sam. 'OK, I promise,' he said, trying to sound pissed off enough for them to think that he meant it.

'But I want to go back there,' Jeff said.

'Kate will take you,' Suzannah said, forever the diplomat.

'I will?' Kate teased.

'But Kate is going on holiday,' Jeff complained.

'Where are you going?' Sam had decided that it was high time to try to change the subject.

'Munich.' Kate glanced at her mother, but she already seemed busy clearing a space on the table for dessert.

'Who are you going with?' Jeff asked. 'With your new *boyfriend*?'

'This one's serious. You wait and see!' Kate said.

'He must be your *tenth* boyfriend this year!' Tony said, and smiled cheekily. 'And it's only August!'

Kate couldn't help laughing. She picked up her knife and fork and pretended to cut a slice off Tony. Jeff laughed. 'Don't you start! I'm going to have fried Jeff for seconds,' she added, moving towards him and making him giggle hysterically.

'Yuck!' Sam exclaimed. She was glad the subject had changed. She and Tony looked at each other. She thought they'd handled it pretty well, all things considered.

5

Kate stood in the doorway of what used to be her and Francesca's room, her head resting against its frame. On it the engravings indicated their heights over the years, at least until Kate was thirteen, when the marks stopped when their dad had died. Tony, Sam and Jeff were sprawled on the floor, playing Memory.

The few toys that had remained on the shelves were Kate and Francesca's, and Kate was a little annoyed that she could not stay in her old room when she came to visit. She was allocated a fold-out bed in the little sitting room on the ground floor at the back of the house and her presence there seemed always inconvenient. It was almost as if her mother didn't want her here.

Not for the first time Kate was surprised the world map that as a teenager she had attached with drawing pins to the ceiling over her bed was still there. She decided that she should take it down, fold it up carefully at the kitchen table, for all to see, then take it with her when she went and so move out for good. The only problem was that once again she had no home to go to. What was it with her with homes and jobs and lovers? Every time she secured one of them, the other two fell by the wayside. It didn't help that as she got older she became more demanding, expected better jobs, better homes and better lovers, unlike her friends who seemed to settle for less, and were still happy with their lot.

When Kate couldn't sleep after her dad had gone, she would look up at the map, aided by the light of the planetarium she had been given one birthday, and think of all the places she could imagine living. As soon as she was old enough to travel on her own, she started to tick off countries from her list.

The one place she had never been to was Germany. Kate had read so much about Germany over the years that she had convinced herself a trip there would never be more than a journey to confirm what she already knew. Six million Jews in three years – that took some effort, Kate thought, not to mention all the others. All that poison gas manufactured, distributed and administered, seemingly by invisible hands.

She knew that genocide wasn't an exclusively German thing, it was just that the Germans had been so much better at it. They built better cars, ran railway networks like clockwork and, while IG Farben and Krupp built fortunes on slave labour, and Volkswagen let their labourers' children die of neglect in 'baby farms', the extermination business went from strength to strength. As far as Kate was concerned only a deserted Germany, its bombed buildings unrepaired, its autobahns deserted, its fauna bursting through the asphalt, would convince her that all the guilty had been punished.

Yet there was something that did not fit. No one could have been more surprised than she at her tears of joy when she saw the first news reports of the Wall coming down. And she had made sure that no one could be more surprised: she had hidden in the bathroom and emerged only when the tears had dried and the newscaster had moved on to something else. She had looked at herself in the bathroom mirror: who was she? She thought she had been thoroughly English, even though her mother had been born in Germany. And maybe the day the Wall came down was when her desire to go to Germany to exorcise her demons first emerged. But it was too soon. She would have to wait until there was no urgency any more, when Germany had settled again and she had someone to hold on to.

She should have gone to Germany many years ago. She could have signed up for a school trip when she was in her early teens – added her name below the inviting notice on the pin board in her school's entrance hall, which had quickly filled up with the names of students less hesitant than she. Or she could have strayed across the border on her one disastrous attempt at a skiing holiday, in the French Alps, when she was in her early twenties. After the first ill-fated morning she had spent the rest of the week with her arm in plaster, wandering between the hotel bar and their room. Germany was only a short bus ride away, but she had avoided even considering a visit, telling herself she actually preferred spending the rest of her holiday reading the second-rate horror novels her then boyfriend had brought along and sipping G&Ts, occasionally glancing surreptitiously at Germany, which lay on the other side of the valley, as if she were nursing a guilty secret.

Kate was glad to be interrupted in her thoughts when Richard appeared next to her in the doorway. Richard took a peek into the room, where the children were getting animated.

'What are you guys playing?' he asked.

'Look!' Jeff said, and picked up a square card that was lying face down on the floor amongst many others. He turned it over: it was a picture of a chicken. He picked up another card: another chicken. He turned a third card, and this time it was a horse. He picked up another card, also a horse, then beamed as he collected up the pairs of cards.

'You're cheating!' Tony said.

'I'm not.'

'How can you cheat at Memory?' Sam asked.

Richard looked at Jeff with what Kate thought was genuine amazement. 'How do you know where the pairs are?'

'I remember them,' Jeff said proudly. 'Whenever someone turns a card you just have to remember what it is.'

'And *where* it is,' Sam added.

Jeff picked up a card of a pig, but this time couldn't find the one that matched.

'You never played this when you were a kid?' Kate asked.

'Nope.'

'Deprived childhood or what?'

'I guess we were too busy setting neighbours' cars on fire,' Richard chuckled.

'I suppose it doesn't rain much in New York.'

'Not in the summer.'

It was Tony's turn. 'I know where it is!' he announced, picking up two cards. He turned both cards back quickly, disappointed.

'Hey, what was that?' Sam shouted. 'I didn't see it!' Tony turned the cards again. One was the missing picture of the pig. When he turned it face down Sam immediately picked up the pair of pigs.

Richard looked on as the children completed the game. When they had finished, they compared the heights of the stacks of the cards they had collected. Jeff was the clear winner.

'Stupid game,' Tony said, and picked himself up off the floor.

6

The knock came a little later than he had expected. Richard had been finding the book he was reading heavy going. Maybe he was suffering from the burden of having taken up a recommendation. Richard always read what people suggested, took it as some sort of duty, but more often than not he turned out to be disappointed. He was only too glad to put the book down on the side table next to him.

Richard had left the door ajar and Robert peeked through the gap. 'Am I disturbing you?' He pushed open the door.

'Nope, come on in. I can't make sense of this thing anyway.' Richard pointed in the direction of the abandoned book, now lying with a pile of others, but vaguely enough, he reckoned, that he wouldn't have to start a conversation about it. He hoped that it hadn't been a book Robert had recommended.

Robert hovered in the vicinity of the table, confused as to which book Richard was talking about. 'How are things with you?' he finally asked.

'Fine. Things are fine.' Richard knew what Robert had

come to talk about, but he'd be damned if he'd make it easy for him.

'I hope the trip works out for her.'

'Why shouldn't it? He sounds nice enough.'

'I don't know. Nice enough doesn't seem nice enough for Kate.'

'She can take care of herself.'

Richard wasn't in the mood for small talk. Especially about Kate. He still considered Robert a stranger, even though Francesca and he had been together for almost twelve years. They had never married, and it didn't look as if they ever would. Discussions with Robert about family went against the grain.

'Did you get my note?' Robert finally asked. Richard thought that, for a journalist, he certainly took his time getting to the point.

'Yes.'

'And?'

'How did you find out?'

'I did my research. I put two and two together.'

'Did you tell Suzannah?'

'She doesn't know?' Richard could make out genuine surprise in Robert's eyes.

'Nope.'

'Well, I won't tell her. This thing is strictly between you and me,' Robert said. 'It wouldn't be ethical.'

'Yeah, you got ethics. I never had ethics.'

'Richard . . .'

'You know, I never knew what ethics meant. Literally,' Richard said. 'Everyone kept talking about ethics. You've got to have ethics, ethics are good, something desirable. But when they taught the word at school I must have been off sick. I never knew what it meant. Not until I was in my early twenties.' Richard laughed. 'You know, I asked a girlfriend once, when I was twenty-two, twenty-three, what ethics meant and she started this whole monologue about what ethics meant to her. I was too embarrassed to tell her that what I was asking for was a definition. Isn't that funny?' Richard looked at Robert but could not make out what he was thinking. 'Anyhow, in the end I looked it up in a dictionary and the whole ethics thing suddenly began to make sense. I always thought it meant courage. Maybe it actually means the opposite. What do you think?'

Robert turned away, and Richard thought maybe he had been too harsh on him. After all, he was only trying to do his job.

'I'm not ready to expose my soul to anyone,' Richard said. 'I don't even expose it to my family.' He added a chuckle to take the edge off what he had just said, hoping that Robert would just take it as a joke.

'Well, maybe you should,' Robert said, and looked Richard in the eye. Richard avoided his gaze and immediately regretted it. He glanced back at Robert, but Robert had already turned away again. Richard realised that they must have had entire conversations without looking each other in the eye.

'You know,' Richard finally said, 'it all seems so trivial, yet it's far from it.'

'That is exactly the kind of thing I'm looking for.'

'For your book.'

'For my book.'

For a moment they fell silent. Richard hoped Robert would just leave. He wanted to be alone to think. What Robert had implied was right. If he didn't pin things down soon, he would forget. He was convinced of that. Robert's note had made him curious. Over the years his recollection of that day had become confused: some of it he could remember as if it were yesterday, other details he could not remember at all, and the longer he thought about it the more uncertain he became about what was real and what was not.

When, three weeks ago, he'd sent off for the tape he'd been sure this was the right thing to do, but now he was no longer certain. If Suzannah saw the package he'd have to explain it, and he couldn't even explain it to himself. She'd probably just shrug it off, but he didn't know whether that wouldn't actually be worse than facing her curiosity.

Richard saw Robert pick up the book he'd been reading, and flick through it. It couldn't have been one he had recommended after all.

'This book you're writing, is anyone going to read it?' Richard asked.

'I hope so.' Robert put the book down again, to Richard's relief.

'Then you can *definitely* count me out.' Richard wondered how Robert got the idea to write the book, and supposed he should ask.

Robert picked up another book at random, looked at it briefly and put it back. Maybe he's more nervous about the whole thing than I am, Richard thought.

'I'm not proud of what I've done,' he said.

'You're talking about yourself as if you were a war criminal.'

'And I wasn't?'

'You were nothing of the sort.'

'I'll be the judge of that.' Richard was agitated but tried his best not to sound it. 'Not you and not whoever reads this thing.'

'Most of us would have done the same. That's the whole point.'

'I had never planned to be most of us.'

Robert had finally stopped eyeing the books and gone to

look out of the window. Richard just hoped he'd go away.

'It's beautiful from up here,' Robert said.

'I don't know. Sometimes I miss the skyscrapers.'

'I wish you'd reconsider.'

'I *have* reconsidered.'

Robert walked to the door and turned round so that he was finally looking at Richard. 'Still, let me know if you change your mind,' he said, and left the room.

7

Kate was surprised to feel her heart pounding as she entered the conservatory. This is it, I am really going, she thought. She had booked tickets to far-flung places without the blink of an eye, but she felt that for a trip to Germany she needed her mother's blessing. She had mentioned her trip to many people but never directly to her mother.

The small conservatory was her mum's territory and this is where she had set up her painting, amongst the random pieces of furniture that had collected here over the years. Her mother had studied art at school but hadn't touched a paintbrush again until she retired. Biology, the subject, and biology, as in having two kids to raise, got in the way. The painting Suzannah was working on faced towards the window and Kate was half expecting her mother to tell her to stop before she could see it, but Suzannah looked up and invited Kate to step closer.

Kate looked at the painting. If I were a painter, I'd hide my work until it was finished, she thought. Lock myself in a room and do whatever I had to do until I was ready to share it with the world, to wild applause or deafening silence.

'So you're off tomorrow?'

'Yes.'

'What's he like?'

'Oh, handsome, charming, fabulous in bed . . .'

'Kate!'

'You did ask.'

'And when did you meet him?'

'Two months ago.'

'And what does he do?'

'Something geeky to do with IT that I haven't quite figured yet.' Kate laughed. 'I'll let you know the minute I do.'

'And do you love him?' Suzannah was never shy to ask questions cutting right to the chase, but Kate was used to it.

Kate hesitated. 'I don't know yet.' He certainly made her feel different from the way she'd felt with the others. When she'd seen him with another woman a few days after their initial meeting, she'd been gripped by a sudden jealousy that she found hard to explain. Even though she had had her fair share of jealous moments, the intensity far outweighed anything she had felt before. Even when it turned out to have been an innocent encounter with a work colleague, Kate could not forget how consumed she'd been by her jealousy. She didn't like the vulnerability Steve had brought her. If she had to feel something like this, she wanted to feel it on her terms.

'And when are we going to meet him?'

'I don't know.' Kate never liked introducing boyfriends to her family in case the relationship self-destructed, as it usually did. Steve and she had planned to have him stay for the few days before the trip, but at the last minute Kate decided that imposing her family plus a week's holiday on him in quick succession might scare him away. 'Maybe after the holiday. I have to see.'

'I hope you're both going to have a nice time.'

'We'll do our best.'

'How are you going to get to the airport?' Suzannah asked.

Kate realised that she hadn't thought about the practical side of things. 'I thought maybe I could borrow the car. Park it at the airport.' Her mum's car seemed to spend most of its time in the garage.

'I'll need the car,' Suzannah said without looking up.

'Maybe you could drive me.' As if a different expression would make a difference, Kate added, 'Give me a lift.'

'I have to be in town by noon.'

'What for?'

'To run an errand,' Suzannah said. 'It's Friday.' Kate didn't want to ask.

Kate thought that maybe that was why her mother and Richard got along so well: they both had their routines and neither included the other.

'How am I going to get to the airport then?'

'Why don't you take the train?'

'That's going to be awkward.'

'You should have thought about that before.'

Kate shrugged. 'It's not my fault that you live in the middle of nowhere.' She regretted that as soon as she'd said it. She was here as a guest while she was sorting her life out, for the umpteenth time. She had moved out of her last boyfriend's flat before Christmas, and had since been alternating between friends' sofas and her mum and Richard's house.

For a while they fell silent, and Kate thought of leaving it at that, packing her things and calling Steve to make the final arrangements.

She looked at her mother's painting and decided that she liked it. If she had a flat of her own, she'd like to put it on the wall, maybe above the chimneypiece. Most of her mum's work ended up in the cellar, never to be seen again. Kate would have expected the house to be full of paintings, but there wasn't a single one of Suzannah's on the walls. Only her work in progress would be on display on the easel until she started another one, as if the finished work meant nothing to her.

Kate could hear the first drops of rain hitting the roof of the conservatory, and realised that she hadn't noticed it had stopped raining.

'Why Germany?' Suzannah finally asked, perhaps sensing that Kate was about to go.

'Why not?'

Suzannah shrugged.

'Because the Germans have done a terrible thing?' Kate asked. 'And fifty years later they are still the bad Germans in your book?'

'Terrible *things*. And not just in my book.'

'I've seen *Schindler's List*.'

'I know you have.' Suzannah started to clean her brush. 'I don't know why you didn't just take my word for it. Why did you have to go and watch a movie about it?' She didn't sound too upset, Kate thought.

'Don't you think it's time to forgive and forget?' Kate was asking a rhetorical question. She knew that there would never be a time for forgetting. After all, that was why she was going. Not to forget, but to remember things she had never known, if that made any sense.

'Forgive, maybe in a hundred years. Forget? Never.'

'You should have come.'

'I don't think Steve would appreciate it.' Suzannah chuckled. There was another thing her mum and Richard had in common when Kate came to think of it: their laughter. They had their own routines, but they laughed together. For a moment she felt a pang of envy.

'You know what I mean. We should have gone a long time ago, just you and I.'

'I don't think that would have been such good idea.'

'But you can't stop me from going.'

Suzannah looked up at Kate. Kate thought she made out genuine surprise in her eyes. 'Of course not. Whatever gave you that idea?'

'I want to see for myself what it's like.'

'They put a number on me.'

Suzannah started to paint again. She added a new colour to what had looked to Kate like an almost completed painting and Kate immediately saw the picture took on a whole new dimension. That's why I would never make a good painter, she thought.

By now the rain was pounding heavily on the roof. If it rained any harder, it would be impossible to talk. Kate had to raise her voice.

'Let me go, Mum.' For a moment she thought that Suzannah hadn't heard, but when she saw her reflection in the windows as she turned to go, she knew she had.

8

Kate didn't know how long she had been in the garden, close to the gate that led out into the forest, next to the pond she used to play by as a child. She had been thinking about her trip, and for a moment she didn't want to go, didn't want to go through the whole hassle of travelling: getting to the airport, flying, checking into a hotel and finding her way around a country she didn't know and whose language she could not speak.

She heard approaching footsteps and turned.

'Good morning.' Richard was approaching behind her, in his dressing gown.

'Oh, hi,' Kate said. 'You're up early.'

'I could say the same about you.'

'I couldn't sleep,' Kate said.

'I generally get up with the sun these days.' Richard said, and Kate realised that she had missed the sun rising. It had still been dark when she woke up, and she had made a quick decision, dressed and gone outside. When she was off work she rarely got up before nine, but somehow she didn't want to miss any moments of her last morning in England. It had stopped raining just before dawn, and she was craving fresh, clean air.

'Remember that?' Kate said, and pointed at a dirty yellow object floating in the middle of the pond, stuck in some muddy leaves. It was her favourite plastic duck, which she had lost one winter and hadn't been allowed to retrieve. Now it was difficult to believe that the shallow water had ever posed a serious threat.

'Nope,' Richard said candidly, and for an instant looked sad. Of course it was long before he came, and Kate kicked herself for being so insensitive. She couldn't remember him ever forbidding her anything.

'Are you looking forward to your trip?' Richard asked.

'No, I'm not,' Kate said quickly, surprising herself with the answer. It was too early in the morning to play games.

'Why not?'

'I don't know. Maybe because Mum doesn't want me to go.'

'Oh, I don't know about that.'

'I do.'

'You know—' Richard said.

'I know.' She was not entirely sure what she was meant to know and was sorry that she had interrupted him. They were quiet for a moment.

For a second Kate felt like just walking into the pond and getting the duck. Her trousers would get wet, and she might have to repack for her trip, but who cared?

'Good luck at the doctor's, by the way,' she said instead. Richard looked a little unsettled. 'Mum told me.'

Richard was going for a check-up Suzannah had said, nothing important, but you never knew at his age, she'd added. Kate wondered whether she was keeping something from her.

'It's just routine,' Richard said.

'I'll call you to check the results,' Kate said. She could

tell that Richard was not as irritated by her concern as he wanted to appear.

'Don't waste your money. I'll be fine.'

'If they do anything unspeakable to you, I'll be on the next plane back to beat them up.' Kate made a fist and an angry face to match it, and Richard laughed.

'I hope there won't be any need for that.'

'I'll bring you back a present,' Kate decided.

'Don't worry about it.'

Kate would get him something really special. To say thanks for the last fifteen years he had taken care of her. They fell silent.

'How are you going to get to the airport?' Richard asked eventually.

'I ordered a cab to take me to the station,' Kate said.

'That'll cost you.'

'Holiday, you know.' Kate shrugged. 'It will pick me up at ten.'

'Will that be enough time?'

'Should be ample,' Kate said, and took Richard's hand a little awkwardly. It felt big and rough, just like she remembered, and she wondered how long it had been since she had held it.

'I love you,' she said, and wasn't quite sure why she had felt it was necessary to put it into words. But now that she had, it felt right.

'I love you, too.' Richard didn't seem as embarrassed as she had thought he might be.

She let go of his hand. 'Take care of yourself.' She smiled. She noticed that Richard had a small packet under his arm, and looked at him questioningly.

'Something I've been meaning to look at for a long time,' he explained, and Kate knew that that was all he was prepared to say about it.

'Dirty video, huh?' she teased.

Richard didn't mind that Kate had spotted it. By the time she had returned he would have told Suzannah, and then he would tell Kate, too. All in his own time. 'You could say that.' Richard seemed to be gripping the packet tighter. Kate saw that he was shivering.

'You'd better go in, you'll catch a cold in this thing,' she said.

'And it's meant to be summer.'

'You're more English than the English,' she said.

'Is that supposed to be a compliment?' Richard asked.

'I don't know.' Kate smiled. 'I'll let you know.'

'And you?' Richard turned to go. 'You coming in? I'll buy you breakfast.'

'I'll stay for another couple of minutes,' she replied.

Richard kissed her on the forehead. 'Fly carefully,' he said, and turned to go back to the house. She looked after him and he gave a slight and awkward wave. She watched him disappear into the house. She too could feel a chill and pulled her cardigan more tightly around her. She looked up at the blue morning sky. It would be a warm day.

In the distance, beyond the forest and above the sea, she could make out the contrail of an aeroplane heading for the sun.

9

Kate felt a slight unease as she saw the houses getting smaller and the cars turn into toys. She wasn't scared of flying exactly but imagined that for something so heavy to stay up in the air required faith, faith she didn't always have. As the British Airways flight from Heathrow to Munich climbed higher, she found it hard to believe that the plane had already made the journey twice that day, and she never.

When the seat belt sign switched off with a friendly ping and an announcement confirmed that they were out of immediate danger, Kate's anxiety eased, but she kept her seat belt on, just in case.

She looked at Steve, who had given her the window seat (passed), carried her bag (passed) and accompanied her to the duty-free perfume counter without much complaining (passed with distinction). They had held hands during take-off, and now, as the seat belt sign suggested, they too released their grip. If anything he had been looking more nervous than she, but was trying not to show it. Kate leaned over and gave him a kiss on the cheek.

'What?' He seemed surprised.

'Nothing.'

Hey, boy, I'm going on holiday with you, she thought. Not for the first time she reminded herself to be good to him. Soon after they had met she had decided Steve was a keeper. He was not like her other boyfriends: he had treated her like a grown-up, was happy just to listen when she needed to be listened to, happy to put up with the issues she was facing – the non-boyfriend-related ones at least – which she carefully unveiled one after another, testing the water, each time feeling that their connection strengthened rather than weakened.

'Would you like something to drink?' the stewardess asked. Kate hadn't noticed her approach.

'Do you have any champagne?' Steve asked.

'Champagne? Are you crazy?' Kate smiled broadly. This man was trying to please her. What on earth was wrong with him?

'We have some sparkling wine. I'll bring it over to you.'

'You only like me because I'm crazy,' Steve said, when the stewardess had turned back to her trolley.

'I do not.'

'Yes, you do.'

'Anyway, you've got it all wrong. You're not crazy,' Kate said. '*That's* why I like you.'

The stewardess returned with two small bottles. They were plastic. Steve reached for his wallet.

'No charge,' she smiled.

Steve put his wallet back, a little embarrassed. So he wasn't such a man of the world after all, Kate thought, and grinned. She'd have to teach him some tricks.

When the stewardess had moved her attention to the next row, he started to shake his bottle. 'It's no fun if it doesn't spill,' he explained.

Kate shrieked and shielded herself with the safety-instruction leaflet. Steve unscrewed the top, but the bottle opened without making so much as a sound. He filled one of the plastic glasses, and gave it to Kate.

'Not so crazy after all, huh?' Kate said, as Steve opened his bottle.

'I guess not.' Steve raised his glass and Kate followed.

'Here's to holiday,' she said.

'To holiday!'

They clinked glasses, but the clink of plastic also left something to be desired. Kate decided that it was the thought that counted.

She had a sip. It tasted good. She looked out of the window, down at the toy version of England, just in time to see the coast appear.

They were jostled under a sign reading 'WELCOME TO GERMANY' and in the direction of passport control by the crowd of businessmen returning home after a day in London. Their fellow travellers were in a controlled hurry – professional commuters – and Kate thought they looked relieved to have returned from the chaos of London into the clean, orderly world of what they called home.

When the crowds became thicker as they approached passport control Steve removed his passport from his bag.

'Let me see your picture!' Kate demanded.

'Oh, no, please, it's awful,' he said, but she was determined to get it off him. He held up the passport in the air and Kate tried to jump for it.

'It can't be that bad,' she said, finally managing to extract it from him. She opened his passport and flicked to the page with his picture. 'You're right, it *is* that bad,' she announced, and he took it back, pretending to be more annoyed than he was.

The queue started to dissolve, and Kate was disappointed to see that everyone was being waved through. No need for passports any more. I wouldn't have minded a stamp in mine, she thought, but we all live in one country now.

At the end of the long corridor after passport control, Kate entered the revolving doors leading to baggage reclaim and pushed the handle, which brought the door to an instant halt. The trickle of businessmen behind them came to a standstill.

An irate man stepped from grey anonymity into her world. 'Didn't you see the sign?' he asked with an anger that was emphasised by his perfect, accent-free English. Later it occurred to her to wonder how he knew that she was English – was it the passport? – yet she knew that she must already have put it away.

She looked for the sign he was referring to, but she must have already passed it. The door started to revolve again. On the other side he melted in with the crowd of men in suits again, being fast-tracked through the blue zone without giving the baggage reclaim area so much as a second glance.

Steve and Kate stayed behind, letting everyone who was in a hurry pass them, and started to look out for their luggage. They were on holiday and had all the time in the world.

10

'How did it get in there?'

'There must be a hole somewhere.'

'How is it going to get out?'

Sam, Tony and Jeff were standing at the fence surrounding the electricity substation. A large brown and black dog with piercing eyes cowered between the two transformers, almost as if it were kept there by the invisible push of the electricity. It seemed unable to move.

'How is it going to get out?' Jeff repeated, tugging at Sam's shirt.

'I'm not sure I *want* it to come out,' Sam said. 'It doesn't look very friendly.' The dog looked as if it would growl at them, were it not too tired and weak. It looked sick, *really* sick. Sam thought it couldn't have eaten for days, judging by its emaciated body.

'There must be a hole somewhere,' Tony said, and started to walk around the fence. 'You go round the other way,' he instructed Sam. 'Be careful.'

'Jeff, you stay here,' Sam said, but Jeff didn't look as if he was going anywhere. He was transfixed by the dog. Sam slowly and carefully checked the fence, walking anticlockwise. If she did find the hole, she was going to be careful, even if Tony had said so. But there wasn't one.

Tony and Sam met up on the other side of the clearing.

'Anything?' Tony asked.

'No.'

'There must be,' Tony said. 'You can't have checked properly.'

'I did,' Sam insisted.

'Let me check your side.'

'And I'll check yours.'

'There's nothing on my side,' Tony insisted.

Sam checked Tony's side as carefully as she had her own. He was right. Nothing. They met up again where they'd started.

'Nothing.'

'Nothing.'

Jeff was still watching the dog. He hadn't taken his eyes from it, nor the dog from him.

'It likes you,' Sam said.

'You think so?' Jeff asked.

'Of course it likes you,' Tony needled. 'It likes you enough to have you for dinner.'

'Stop it,' Sam said, but was too occupied with the mystery of how the dog had got in there to get worked up about her brother's teasing.

'It must have got in through the gate,' she finally decided.

'What? Do you think it came with its own key?'

'No, silly,' Sam said. 'Someone must have locked it in there.'

'Why would someone do something like that?' Jeff asked.

'Beats me.'

'I don't think anyone locked it in here.' Tony had walked over to the gate. 'Take a look.'

Sam examined the big padlock that fastened the perimeter fence's only gate. It was rusty and didn't look as if it had been opened for years. She cautiously pushed the gate. The rust had stuck it to its frame.

'No one's been through this for a while,' Tony said.

'What if it jumped from a tree or something?' Jeff suggested.

'Dogs don't climb trees, stupid!' Nevertheless Tony looked around – there were no branches close enough to have been used as a springboard.

'But it must have got in somehow!' Sam said.

'And how is it going to get out?' Jeff asked, his eyes still on the dog.

Tony looked at Sam. She could recognise that look immediately. He had found a new challenge. Even she had to admit that it wasn't a bad one.

'Jeff's right,' Tony said. 'We've got to get it out somehow. Otherwise it will die.'

'We should tell someone,' Sam suggested quickly.

'Who's going to believe us? We're kids,' Tony said. 'And, anyhow, we're not supposed to be here.'

'We can get Granddad to call the police,' Sam said. 'We can get him to come down here. He won't tell on us, and they'll believe him.'

'And then what? Nobody cares about dogs,' Tony said. 'They'll take the dog away and shoot it. Do you want it to be shot?'

'They don't shoot dogs any more,' Sam insisted.

'No, they put them to sleep,' Tony said quickly. 'Do you want it to be put to sleep?'

'No,' Sam said quietly. 'Of course not.' She wasn't crazy about dogs, and she was sure dogs weren't too crazy about her either, but she certainly didn't want to be responsible for one being killed. After all, it had been someone's puppy once, however viciously it might be looking at them now. If it weren't for the fence, Sam was convinced the dog would attack them. But, still, it had the right to live.

'It's up to us to save it,' Tony said, looking at Sam expectantly.

'And how are we supposed to do that?' she asked, although she thought he had a point. They would have to get the dog out of there somehow – and hope that it wouldn't set on them. As if in response, the dog managed a quiet growl. She hoped it had a home to go to, but noticed that it didn't have a collar.

'It looks hungry,' Jeff said. He turned to Sam. 'We've got to feed it.'

'Let's find it something to eat,' Tony decided.

'Where are we going to get food from?' Sam asked.

'Jeff can figure it out. It was his idea.' Tony looked at Jeff.

'We'll ask Grandma,' Jeff said.

'And tell her what?' Tony asked. 'Tell her that we've gone back to the place we're not supposed to go and are going to feed a vicious dog? No, we've got to take something without them finding out.'

'You mean steal it?' Jeff asked.

'We wouldn't exactly be stealing,' Tony grinned at Jeff. 'You'd just have to take it.'

'Me?' Jeff asked.

'Yes, you! Don't you want us to take you more seriously?' Tony said.

Jeff looked at Sam, but she turned away. She didn't want to take food she wasn't supposed to, but she could see no other solution.

11

After dinner Richard closed the door of his study and walked over to his desk. He kneeled down on the floor and crawled under the kneehole. With some effort he pushed open the drawer on the other side from underneath. The desk had been in this room for ever, even before Suzannah bought the house. It had been designed for two people, one sitting on either side, with a set of drawers for each user. For each accessible drawer on the side Richard used, there was another on the opposite side. Most could not be opened at all as they were right up against the wall, others could only be opened a little, and the middle, large but shallow one, could be pushed out almost halfway until it rested against the bay window.

Once he had pushed the middle drawer as far as it would go, he got out from underneath the desk, and brushed the dust off his clothes. He leaned across the desk to retrieve the videotape. His heart was racing, and he counted himself lucky that no one had come in to disturb him. The key to his study had long been missing and, anyway, he would find a locked door more difficult to explain than whatever he got up to under his desk.

The tape had finally appeared that morning on the doormat. He had been so surprised to see Kate standing outside that he had forgotten to hide the tape when he had gone to join her. And somehow he didn't mind Kate knowing, sure that she would not press him to explain.

After he had seen Kate he had taken the tape to his study and examined the familiar US stamps, then turned the package in his hands for any more signs of home. He had contemplated opening the package there and then, but thought better of it. Suzannah could wake at any moment – he'd decided to return to bed after all.

Watching the sun crawl up the bedroom wall, he'd been sure that he wouldn't be able to go back to sleep again, and was surprised when he woke up two hours later, long after Suzannah had got up. He hurried to get dressed, in the back of his mind suspecting that his package had been found and opened. The whole family would be downstairs in the living room, watching the tape. They would turn to look at him as he walked tiredly down the stairs and ask him: 'Was that really you? Was it you who did this thing?' And perhaps that would have been the best way: have it out in the open without his having prepared an answer. Talk it through, explain what there was to be explained and maybe then he would be able to sleep better every morning, not just this one day.

Now he used his letter-opener, but the package was too well sealed and he had to force it open with his hands. Some of the packaging spilled on the floor and Richard was careful to pick it all up and throw it into the bin. Reaching inside, he pulled out a VHS videotape. It was unlabelled, but a sheet of paper confirmed that it was what he had ordered. He was breathing heavily. Should he watch it now? This seemed as good a time as any, but he hesitated.

He had an old video recorder here in his study, hooked

up to an even older TV. He always had a blank tape to hand just in case there was something interesting on he could tape and show to his grandchildren the following day, but they'd say, 'Oh, that, Granddad, that's so last year,' or, the phrase that always killed him, 'That's for kids.' Nevertheless, he kept trying, and anyway, if he didn't satisfy his grandchildren's curiosity, he satisfied his own.

Richard looked at the tape and was about to put it into the video recorder when he heard a stifled laugh emanating from somewhere behind the sofa. He pretended not to hear it, and placed the tape back in its envelope then casually put it on his desk as if it were just another piece of mail.

Richard stretched his arms. 'What should I do now?' he said to himself. 'I wonder where the children are. It's so peaceful and quiet. Maybe I'll just sit down and read a little.'

He picked up a book at random and moved to sit in his armchair. As soon as he had sat down the deafening sound of a whoopee cushion filled the room and the sniggering from behind the sofa turned into outright laughter. Richard got up again as quickly as he had sat down and pretended to be annoyed.

'What on earth . . . !'

'Gotcha, Granddad.' Jeff emerged with a beaming smile from behind the sofa. Tony and Sam followed. Sam had a hunch that Granddad was playing along with them, but that never lessened her enjoyment of these pranks.

Tony walked up to Richard, putting on a solemn face. 'We're really sorry, Granddad,' he said, and reached out his hand in a conciliatory gesture. 'Let me apologise.'

Richard accepted his hand generously but quickly withdrew it when he received a small shock. When he let go, the toy Tony had hidden in his hand fell on the floor and continued its buzzing for a second or two.

'Gotcha again, Granddad!' Tony shouted, and ran away. Richard pretended to be very angry and started to chase the children around the room.

'I'm going to get you for this,' he growled, but already the children were catching up on him on the second lap around the sofa. 'I'm going to get you!' he shouted again, and bared his teeth. Jeff screamed with delight. But soon Richard had to slow down. He was glad when the children let themselves fall on to the sofa, and he joined them, exhausted.

Sam was curled up on the sofa like a cat, listening to Richard reading her a story. *The Little Prince* was Richard's favourite book, he had told her, and every time he read it he discovered something new, peeling away another layer he had not thought of before. She liked the stories, and the rhythm of Richard's voice had almost turned it into a song.

The little prince had arrived on a planet with a street light and a lamplighter, whose sole job it seemed was to light and put out the street light. The little prince tried to find out why, but the lamplighter didn't know. 'Orders are orders,' the lamplighter insisted.

When the lamplighter had put out the lamp yet again, despite the little prince's incessant questions, Richard paused and the fire in the fireplace crackled comfortingly. Richard seemed always to light the fire, Sam thought, no matter how hot or cold it was outside. The first time he had lit it, Grandma had told her, he had forgotten to open the flue and had almost set the house on fire. The whole study had filled with smoke and if you smelled his books closely, they still gave off the aroma of smoke.

Sam liked it here. Richard's study was a place you could always come to and feel safe. Nothing ever changed here.

Well, at least it hadn't as long as she could remember. She found it hard to imagine that someone else had lived here and used these rooms as their home, and that many years from now someone else would use it, and the books would be gone.

'Granddad?' she asked.

'Yes?'

'Why don't you have your own grandchildren?'

Richard laughed. 'Because I didn't have any children.'

'Must be very lonely without children.'

'Well, I've got you, haven't I?'

'But it's not the same, is it?' Sam said, and Richard seemed to consider. That was one of the things Sam liked about her granddad: he always thought about what she had to say.

'I wouldn't have been a good father.'

'Oh, you're the best granddad in the world, even if you're not a real one,' Sam said. 'I'm sure you would have been a great dad as well.'

'Well, thank you.'

They were quiet for a while and Richard picked up the book again.

'Granddad?'

'Yes?'

'That lamplighter, was he happy?'

'I don't know.' Richard seemed startled by Sam's question. 'I suppose so. Why not?'

'What would have happened if he just sat down and didn't do anything?' Sam asked.

'I suppose he would have got bored.'

'He could have made up stories of his own.'

'Maybe.' Richard put the book down again.

'I think I would have just stopped doing it.'

'But if it was an order?'

'I don't know. Who gave the order? Whoever it is, he's

not on the planet any more. The lamplighter is on his own.'

'But the person might come back.'

'What if they're dead?'

'Don't you think an order is still an order? The order has to make sense to someone at some stage. No one gives orders they don't think are good ones, do they?' Sam thought that Granddad sounded a little bitter.

'Then I'd start again. If he came back.' Sam listened to the fire and suddenly felt a chill.

'Another chapter tomorrow?' Richard asked.

Sam felt that her granddad wasn't happy with her answer.

'OK.' Sam got up and gave Richard a kiss and a seven-second hug that lasted more like ten. She walked to the door then turned round.

'Granddad?'

'Mmm?'

'Do you like dogs?'

'Sure, why?'

'You'd feed one if it was hungry?'

'Sure. Why not?' Richard said. 'What dog?'

'Any dog.'

'Sure.'

Sam left, and soon Richard could hear her running down the stairs. He picked up the book he had selected at random and flicked through the pages, but then remembered the videotape, which was still lying on his desk. He got up with some effort, replaced it in the drawer, and climbed under the desk to pull it shut.

12

'Welcome to Germany,' Steve said, and Kate laughed. As he was rolling off her sweaty body she thought that sex was always better somewhere else. On holiday. Or was it really he that made it good?

'Thank you,' Kate smiled, and snuggled into his chest. She looked at the hotel room they had entered just ten minutes ago. Only now did she register the TV, the small fridge and the table with the writing desk. Who writes letters in hotel rooms? she wondered.

'We've got it good, haven't we?' Steve said, kissing the top of her head.

'Oh, yes.' If she could, she'd crawl right under his skin. Steve seemed perfect. She hadn't found a fault yet and that wasn't for lack of trying.

'I love you with so much of my heart that none is left to protest,' Kate quoted, just trying the words out for size, though she found it easier to aim them at the ceiling rather than at Steve. 'I always wanted to say that.' Observing him out of the corners of her eyes she couldn't decide whether he looked worried or not.

'Peter Gabriel?' he teased.

'What? No . . . Shakespeare.' Kate laughed. 'What's the time?'

Steve checked his wristwatch on the bedside table. 'Late in Germany. Early in England,' he said, and showed it to Kate. She hadn't noticed that he had taken off his watch before making love and was a little disappointed that he had thought of it in the heat of their passion.

'Is it true?' Steve asked.

'Is what true?'

'You know, the Shakespeare thing.'

'Almost,' Kate decided.

'Almost?'

'Almost.'

'Well, almost is good enough for me. For now.' Steve put his watch on.

'What do you mean, for now?' Kate grabbed her pillow and started to hit him with it.

'I give up, let me go.' Steve was trying to defend himself but failing miserably. Kate was on top of him, and she could feel that he was turned on again.

'What do you want to do tonight?' she said, then started kissing him hard on the mouth.

'I don't know . . . Whatever you want.'

'You tell me. I am on holiday, I don't want to think.'

Steve pulled her towards him.

Even though Kate would have gladly stayed in bed, she knew Germany was waiting outside asking to be explored. They got dressed and she was happy to venture out into the street to take a look.

The hotel, which they had picked for its location rather than comfort, had its small entrance between two department stores on a pedestrianised shopping street. As they emerged through the glass doors only a handful of people were in the street – the shops had closed.

They decided just to go for a walk and explore the vicinity. After they passed the train station, the luxury shops gave way to more ordinary ones with apartments above. Kate and Steve had passed a handful of sex shops, and Kate was amused by Steve trying to ignore them. They realised that they hadn't eaten since getting on the plane, and bought a couple of rolls with bratwurst from a sausage stand. They stood at a high table beside the snack wagon to eat them.

'Have you ever been in one of those things?' Kate asked between bites, pointing at a peep-show on the other side of the street. Loud rock music pounded through the thick red curtain and out into the summer evening.

'Me?'

'Of course you.'

Steve took a bite, and suddenly seemed to become interested in the pattern of the pavement.

'So, have you?' Kate asked.

'Yes.'

'When?'

'When I was very young.'

'How old?' Kate teased. 'Eight? Nine?'

'A little older than that.' Steve smiled shyly, then took another bite of his roll.

'You *are* very young.' Steve was three years younger than she, which at first she had thought would be a problem.

'When I didn't have you.'

'Oh, yeah?' Kate shouted in mock disgust. 'You need me only for sex, do you?'

'That's not what I meant. I didn't put that right.' He looked genuinely taken aback.

'You can say that again.' Even though Kate had only pretended to be angry, she felt that a little part of her really was hurt. What if it were true?

'Sorry,' Steve said. His face was flushed and he looked contrite. Kate thought how easy he was to manipulate.

Kate saw a man emerge from the peep-show through the curtain. She had finished her food and wiped her hands with the paper napkin that had wrapped the bread. 'Let's try it.' She looked Steve dead in the eye.

'What?'

She pointed in the direction of the peep-show. 'Let's go.'

'You're not serious?'

'Why not?' Even though it was only meant to be a challenge for Steve, she had to admit that she was a little turned on by the idea.

'It's your holiday.' He shrugged.

Steve's indifference was clearly an act, but Kate decided to see how far she could push him. 'That's the spirit.' She took his hand and led him in the direction of the entrance.

Now that he had agreed – a little too easily, to her mind – Kate wasn't quite so sure it was a good idea. She had hoped that he'd spend more time trying to dissuade her. After they had crossed the street, Steve let go of her hand, moved ahead of her and disappeared behind the curtain.

Kate pushed the curtain aside and followed. They had entered a large hall, a round circle of cabins dominating its centre. There were several men hanging around in the vicinity, ignoring the shop window of pornographic videos for sale, and looking as if they were waiting for something to happen. She was relieved that no one looked at her. But why should they? she thought. It wasn't as if they hadn't seen a woman before. A bored-looking attendant sat behind a newspaper. He hardly bothered to glance up.

Steve had stopped in the middle of the room. He looked horribly awkward, and Kate almost felt sorry for him. She couldn't really imagine him coming here on his own. Maybe he had just been showing off?

'So, how do these things work?' she asked, for something to say. It seemed pretty obvious to her.

'Let's see whether we have any change,' Steve said, rummaging through his pockets. He retrieved a small heap of unfamiliar coins and flicked through them. She could see his hand trembling. She looked up at his face to try to figure out what he might be thinking. 'Here,' he said, and attempted to hand her a small heap of euros. 'I'll wait here.'

'Oh no, you won't,' Kate said. 'You're coming with me.' There was no way she would go into one of these cabins on her own. 'I want to keep an eye on you.'

Steve pointed at a sign. As everywhere in Munich so far, there was an English version: 'ONLY ONE PERSON PER CABIN'.

'We're not allowed to go in there together,' he said.

Kate hated to think what people could get up to in a cabin together. Or did they really share to save themselves some money?

'Come on. Don't be such a wuss.' She took Steve's hand again. 'What can they do? Arrest us and throw us into two-persons-in-a-cabin prison?' If she were honest, she wanted to get out of the place as quickly as possible, but she was not prepared to capitulate. Before she could think any more about it, she pulled him towards one of the furthest cabins.

The cabin was small and would hardly hold more than one person anyway; two people only if they were very close. Kate got in and drew Steve in after her. She saw the attendant watching them briefly from over his newspaper, but he looked down again, disinterested. She shut the door and the cabin became dark, illuminated by only a faint red light. The air was stale and had a slight smell of dust and sweat.

'What now?' she asked.

'Money,' Steve said. He handed her the coins, and this time she accepted them. 'All right.' He pointed at an illuminated slot in the corner. 'If you're sure, put it in there.' Kate noticed a dirty tissue on the floor and immediately blocked it out of her mind.

She pushed one of the coins into the slot. Immediately a shutter opened with a whirring sound, revealing a naked woman on a revolving stage. If it hadn't been for the glass she'd almost be close enough to touch. Kate wanted to take a step back, but of course the cabin was too small. The woman danced with mechanical movements to the same rock music that could be heard on the street.

'Can she see us?' Kate whispered to Steve. She fixed her gaze on the woman's body, not daring to look into her face.

'I hope not,' Steve said. He sounded uncomfortable. His arm was touching Kate's, but even though outside in the street she had been turned on by the idea, sex was the last thing she was thinking about now. Finally she dared to lift her eyes to the dancer's face. She looked bored.

It already seemed to Kate as if they had been there an eternity, but the shutter was still up. She wished that it would close. She wanted to look at Steve but wasn't sure how she would deal with it if she saw desire in his eyes. Instead she clung closer to him, wondering whether there had been a mistake, and the shutter was broken. They would have to stand here for ages until someone noticed.

She had seen enough. She looked up at the dancer again, who was still making her bored erotic movements, then thankfully the shutter at last whirred back into action, the window closed and the cabin became dark again.

*

They left the peep-show in silence, walking past the attendant, past the booth where you could get change, past the windows displaying dirty videos, back through the red curtain and out into the street. They kept walking, taking no direction in particular.

Kate breathed a sigh of relief when the music began to fade behind them. Even though she felt that she should make light of their adventure as quickly as possible, she couldn't. They walked in silence for a few blocks until they found themselves clearly moving away from the centre of town, and a decision had to be made where to head next.

They decided to go back to the hotel. To return to the main shopping street they had to walk through the red-light district again. The sex shops they passed no longer felt alluring to Kate, just rather sordid. At a street corner Kate saw a woman smoking a cigarette. A prostitute? How would she feel if Steve paid for sex? That terrible twinge of jealousy she had felt when she'd seen him with the woman from his workplace, was it because she thought his heart belonged to someone else, or his body?

When they were back among the familiar shops, Kate took hold of Steve's hand. She realised that she hadn't held it since the peep-show. From now on she would hold it as often as she could. He was hers and she had better hold on to him.

They stopped in a small twenty-four-hour shop to buy postcards even though Kate had no desire to write any. She spotted a rack with maps of Munich but didn't feel like telling Steve that they needed one. There would be a free one at the hotel anyway, she presumed; all they'd have to do was ask.

After they had paid and left the shop, Kate took Steve's hand again. She looked up at him. He really is not half bad, she thought.

'What?' Steve asked kindly. She felt that he too was snapping out of their pervading pensive mood.

'Nothing,' Kate said. She thought they should talk about their experience at the peep-show. 'Did you think she was beautiful?'

'Who?'

'The woman you just saw naked!'

He shrugged. 'Not as beautiful as you,' he said, and Kate knew he wasn't just being diplomatic. She had expected the dancer to be much more beautiful.

They had arrived on the main pedestrian street and Kate looked around. 'Where is Marienplatz?'

'We should have got a map,' Steve said. The streets had become busier with young people out on the town for the evening. 'I think the hotel is this way.' He pointed in the opposite direction to which they had been walking.

'Are you sure?' Kate smiled.

'No.'

'*That's* what I like about you,' she said, and hooked herself into his arms. She would have gone in any direction he had suggested.

13

'Whoever steps on the white tiles is dead,' Tony announced, and jumped from his place on the second step of the staircase on to the chequered floor of the corridor leading to the entrance hall. He hit a black tile and made his way across the hallway as quickly as possible. He had reached the kitchen in no time and looked back at Sam and Jeff, satisfied. Outside, it was raining and they hadn't mentioned the dog once, even though Sam knew they were all thinking about it.

'You're next,' he said to Sam.

'That's easy.' Sam jumped down from the third step, just to spite him, and ran casually along the hallway, pretending to dance. She didn't hit a white tile once. When she reached the other side, Tony was more than a little miffed.

It was Jeff's turn now, and even he managed the short journey without any mistakes. Tony would have to make the challenge harder, Sam thought.

'OK: now with eyes closed,' Tony announced. 'Give me a scarf.'

Sam looked through the clothes hanging on the coat stand, found a nice scarf and handed it to Tony.

'Not this one, stupid. You can see through that.' Sam took it back, embarrassed, and put it on the stand. She picked one of Granddad's dark brown ones. That would do the trick.

Tony looked at it carefully. 'I suppose it will have to do,' he announced. 'Put it on.'

She tied the scarf around Tony's head, and he adjusted it with his hands. She was sure that he could see out from under it but she didn't say anything.

'Ready?' Sam asked.

'Ready,' Tony confirmed. 'Lead me to the stairs.' Sam took his arm and Tony pretended to be completely blind. When he walked theatrically into the banister, with a mock cry of pain, Sam knew for sure that he was faking.

Tony jumped down on to the black tile. 'See if I can remember.' He jumped again, landing on another black tile, then another and then another.

'Bingo!' he announced, as he reached the other side. 'Now you.'

Sam had to tie the scarf around her eyes herself, and Tony inspected it carefully. 'Hey, you can see through there,' he said, and pulled the scarf further down. He led Sam to the stairs, and she really did hit the banister. It hurt, and she couldn't see a thing.

'Ready?'

'Ready,' Sam confirmed in an uncertain voice, and jumped. When Tony didn't protest she knew that she must have landed on a black tile. She tried to remember how far they were spaced apart and took another jump. Again, not a word from Tony. Sam was getting more confident and jumped another couple of times until the sound changed and she knew that she was on the kitchen's linoleum floor. She pulled down the scarf and beamed in Tony's direction.

'Beginner's luck,' said Tony, clearly annoyed.

'Bah. At least I didn't cheat,' she declared.

'What are you saying? That I didn't play fair?'

'It's my turn.' Jeff tugged at Sam's shirt.

'OK.' She untied the scarf and started to put it on Jeff, but Tony was already on his way up the stairs to his and Jeff's room.

'Let's do something else,' he announced, already halfway up.

'But it's my turn,' Jeff said.

'Come on. Let's go up,' Sam said. 'Some other time.'

14

'Where are you taking me?' Kate asked.

'It's not far,' Steve said. 'In fact, it should be somewhere around here.'

They had spent the last couple of days ticking off tourist sites, but Kate had become bored. That's not what she had come here for, she had told Steve, and she thought that he was as restless as she was.

'There it is.'

'I should have known it would have something to do with drink,' Kate said, laughing, as she saw the blue illuminated neon sign of the Hofbräuhaus.

'I think this may be what you are looking for.'

'I am?'

'Hitler used to come here.'

'Hitler got drunk here? How do you know?'

'He didn't get drunk. And I did some reading before I came.' Steve took her by the hand. 'He gave some of his speeches here.'

He pushed open the entrance door. A staircase led into the basement and as they descended the sounds of music and voices grew louder.

They entered a big hall, with row after row of tables at which people sat talking loudly and drinking from huge glasses.

'Let's go and find a table.' Steve almost had to shout to make himself heard.

'Yeah, let's go and get drunk,' Kate said to herself, and followed him to the back of the hall where there were fewer people.

They found a place on a bench at a large table right next to the kitchen. There were mainly tourists with their cameras at the table, but a few Germans had strayed there, too.

A gesture took care of their order. They didn't have to wait long before their beer arrived. Massive glasses, which Kate calculated held a litre of beer each. The waitress put theirs down along with five others for the people at their table. Steve made to take his, but Kate grabbed both glasses and tried to lift them with one hand. She could only raise them an inch before she had to give up. Laughing, she pushed one of the glasses over to Steve then grasped her glass with both hands.

'Here's to holiday,' she said.

'Holiday.'

'May it not be the last.' They clinked glasses.

'The eternal optimist.' Steve took a sip.

'You know, I never really worked at relationships. I gave up too quickly. I just think I was expecting too much.'

'And now you've got me!'

'I didn't mean it like that,' Kate smiled. 'I just mean I won't let you get away that easily.'

'That's reassuring.'

'It's meant to be,' Kate said, lifting her glass again. It wasn't getting any lighter. The glass itself was a fair weight. They each took a long sip. Kate enjoyed the noise, and took a glance around the room. She was about to turn to Steve when she realised that the man next to them was trying to talk to him. She took an instant dislike to him; couldn't he see that they were too busy with each other to talk to strangers?

'*Ihr erstes Mal hier bei uns?*' the man next to Steve asked.

'*Wie bitte? Ich nicht verstehen* . . . English,' Steve said. Kate was half impressed.

'Is it your first time in Munich?' the stranger asked.

'Yes.'

'I am Johannes and this is my friend Rainer.'

They shook hands. Kate was glad that she didn't have to shake this stranger's hand, as he and his friend were sitting too far away.

'I am Steve and this is my girlfriend, Kate,' Steve said.

Girlfriend. That expression killed Kate every time. That there should be people who wanted her as a girlfriend and would admit it in public still seemed astonishing to her. It was a much better word than 'lover', 'wife' or, even worse, 'partner'. If I want a partner I'll go into business, she thought, but maybe marriage was just that.

'Do you like it here?' The stranger was talking to Kate now, and she had to strain to hear him.

'So far, yes.' And that was true. So far she hadn't seen anything to dislike apart from the business creep at the airport. And she couldn't even be sure that he had been German. It suddenly occurred to her that he might have been English. Why not? He had spoken English without an accent and could have been arrogant enough to assume that everyone understood him.

'Where do you come from?'

'The south-west of England,' Kate said. 'But my mother was born here.'

'So you have German blood.'

'No, my mother is Jewish. So am I, I suppose.'

'You can be both Jewish and German.'

'Nowadays, yes.'

'Kate.' Steve put his hand on her thigh, and for just a second she hated being touched by him.

'No, don't worry, I understand. We don't have much to be proud of,' the German, Johannes, said and briefly looked at his friend.

'That was all a long time ago,' Steve said in a conciliatory tone. He had taken his hand off Kate's thigh, maybe sensing her discomfort, but she reached for it and put it back. He had only meant well.

'Oh, fifty, sixty years is not so long,' Johannes said.

'A lot of things can change in fifty years,' Steve said.

'Yes, but only if you *want* them to change,' Johannes said.

He was certainly not the kind of German Kate had expected. Maybe some of them were planted by the tourist office in every restaurant to talk to visitors – the ones who looked as if they were here to judge – and take the wind out of their sails. Maybe those who had failed the airport test with the revolving door.

'When you English and the Americans came and won the war in 'forty-five,' he continued, 'everyone thought we Germans would change overnight. From murderers and Nazi sympathisers to holy people who would never harm a fly. But why should we change? Just because we see some pictures in the newspapers and hear stories about how evil we were? I don't know how people can expect others to change that easily.'

'But it's not like you're hiding it,' Steve said. 'You are talking about it all the time, trying to remember, so it can't ever happen again.'

'But it can happen again, anywhere, any time.' Kate was

almost shouting to make herself heard over the noise, but also because she was getting angry. And she didn't want to run the risk of having to repeat herself. 'It is happening now.'

'Your girlfriend is right.'

'But not in Germany,' Steve said, and turned to Kate. 'It won't happen again here, right?'

'Didn't you listen to what the man said?' Kate said.

'Calm down.'

'I'm sorry,' Kate said, loud enough for the stranger to hear.

'Don't be sorry. Have a nice stay,' the German said, turning to his friend. '*Zum Wohl.*'

He said a few words to Rainer that Kate couldn't make out, and the friend laughed. She noticed him glancing at her, and she looked away. She wanted to go, but their glasses were still three-quarters full.

'I don't know why I was so aggressive,' Kate said, as they walked back out on to the street. They could drink only half their beers, and had left as soon as they could. 'It's not his fault.'

'He didn't seem to take it the wrong way.'

'I'm sorry.' She held Steve's hand tightly, not so much for comfort but as if she wanted to keep herself from falling off the planet. 'I didn't want to spoil things. Tomorrow we're just going to have fun.'

'You're not spoiling things,' he said, but Kate could see from his expression that she might have done.

'I really don't know why I feel so aggressive here.' Kate wanted to do something for the children of this country. She wanted to help them start anew, with all the information but without the guilt. She thought guilt was a double-edged sword. After a while guilt could turn into defiance, and everything could start all over again.

'It must be strange for you, coming here.'

'I never felt more like a stranger anywhere,' Kate said. 'I have nothing in common with these people.'

'That guy wasn't so bad, was he?' Steve asked gently.

'No.' Kate knew that he was right. He hugged her tight, and Kate felt better than she had felt in a long time. In the embrace of lovers the universe is crushed.

'Let's go back,' Steve said when he let her go.

'To England?' Kate looked at him, surprised, and was curiously happy. They'd have to buy new plane tickets, but what the hell.

'To the hotel, silly.'

'But it's not even ten.'

'I'll think of something to do.'

'You will?' Kate looked at him seductively.

15

The waiting room smelled of death. Not quick death, Richard thought, but slow death from too much alcohol, too many cigarettes and too much junk food. Richard had flirted with all in equal measure, but as he became older his desire for overindulgence diminished.

He took a long look at the other patients. Every time he came here fewer and fewer younger people could be seen in the waiting room. Richard guessed they moved to London as soon as they were old enough. Wasn't that what Kate and Francesca had done?

The number turned on the counter on the wall, and once again Richard had to check his little yellow slip of paper. He had been kept waiting for almost half an hour, but he didn't mind. Now it was his turn and he found his head racing. He got up and wearily took the few steps past reception to the doctor's room.

'Hello. How are you?' Graham said, looking up at Richard as if greeting an old friend. One thing he liked about his doctor was that he always seemed to have all the time in the world. Annoying when you had to wait for half an hour staring at a coloured piece of paper, but you felt you'd hit the jackpot when you finally got to see him.

'Fine.'

'Take a seat,' Graham said, and Richard sat down gratefully. Graham retrieved Richard's file from a pile on the side of the desk and flicked through the notes. Richard realised that he must have known him for the best part of fifteen years. He had been a young, bright spark who took over the practice soon after Richard had moved here, and for a while Richard had felt a great affinity for him. They had almost gone out for a beer together once, but somehow it had never happened.

Graham's perusal of the notes was taking too long for Richard's liking. Maybe it *was* something serious. He should have told Suzannah the whole story, not fobbed her off with a vague tale of some age-related tests. Then she would be here with him, and they'd be facing the bad news together. They'd sit here next to each other, holding hands, as Graham would tell him the implications, not beating about the bush, but with as much kindness as he could muster in front of a dying man. Without Suzannah present, Richard would just have to try to remember all the technical terms for whatever was wrong with him and tell her about it. He wished he had brought a pencil and paper. He guessed he could ask Graham. If the news was bad Graham would get pretty much whatever Richard wanted for him.

Graham looked up. 'All good.' He flicked through another couple of pages. 'Nothing in here that worries me. You do not have dementia.'

Richard was surprised that the relief he felt was mixed with a little disappointment. All this for nothing? 'But what about the test?'

'We've done the blood test and the cognitive tests and there is nothing wrong with you.'

'But the test?'

'It's not an exam. The test shows that you can't remember everything. You're getting older,' Graham said. 'Who isn't?'

'But why can't I remember things?' Richard asked. 'Important things.'

'You're fine,' Graham said. 'With dementia you often can remember perfectly well what you did thirty years ago, but you can't remember what you had for breakfast.'

Richard hesitated.

'Go home.' Graham pretended to push the button of the intercom. 'Nurse, get me some sick people in here.'

Richard laughed as best as he could.

When Richard returned home he knocked at the door to the conservatory.

'Hi,' Suzannah said.

'It turned out to be nothing.'

'See, I told you so,' Suzannah said.

'I should call Kate. She seemed to be interested.'

'Tell her when she comes back.'

'I suppose it can wait.' Richard wouldn't have minded speaking to Kate, but he supposed she wouldn't be at her hotel anyway, and that all he would be able to do was leave a message.

'Tea?'

'No, thank you.' Richard immediately regretted having said no. He looked at Suzannah. I wish you could read my mind, he thought. I would love to tell you about that day, only it's getting harder the longer I leave it.

'Bob called for you,' Suzannah said.

'Bob?' Richard couldn't remember any Bob.

'Robert,' Suzannah smiled.

Francesca's husband. Sometimes Richard felt as if they were all laughing behind his back. Suzannah handed him a

Post-it note, one of the bright yellow ones he hated. 'Here is his number at the paper.'

'What did he want?' Richard asked.

'He didn't say.'

Richard contemplated the telephone in his study and pulled himself together. He straightened out the Post-it note on his desk. She had filled in the 'o' in Bob with a smiley face, and Richard wondered what possessed her to do that.

Richard picked up the receiver and listened for the dialling tone. He dialled the number slowly, but made a mistake and quickly hung up again. He hated making telephone calls. He always felt that he was disturbing people.

He dialled again. Why hadn't Suzannah asked Robert what he was calling him about? The phone was answered almost immediately.

'Robert Banks, please,' Richard said.

'Just a moment,' the man on the other end said. He sounded harassed. Richard looked up at the wall clock and guessed he must have called around press time. He could picture the rows of desks with journalists trying to put tomorrow's paper together.

'Yes?' The brief answer came sooner than Richard had expected.

'Hello.' Richard didn't know how he should introduce himself.

'Richard,' Robert said. 'Good of you to call back.'

'I got your message. What can I do for you?'

'Well, nothing really. I just wanted to tell you . . .' Robert's voice faded away. Richard could hear people shouting in the background. Robert came back to the phone. 'Sorry, it's a madhouse here.'

'I'm sorry.'

'No, I asked you to call. I wanted you to know . . . I just phoned to tell you that the book's been cancelled.'

'Cancelled?'

'Yes, cancelled.' Robert sounded calm considering the hectic activity going on around him. 'The publishers have been bought by some media giant. My editor's gone and the book's been cancelled. I found out last night. I called you as soon as I could.' When Richard took his time to reply, he added: 'They're no longer interested.'

'I'm sorry,' Richard said, thinking that in some way he *was* sorry.

'Well, I thought you'd want to know. I thought it might come as a relief to you.'

It suddenly occurred to Richard that Robert might respect him. Why hadn't he realised that before? 'Yes, thank you,' he said. 'That is a relief.' But if it was, why didn't it feel like it?

Robert didn't say anything and for a moment Richard thought he had hung up.

'I am sorry,' Robert said finally.

'And are you still interested?' Richard asked. He could make out a sigh.

'Certainly I am, Richard,' Robert said. 'But I have to pay the bills. They offered me a contract to write a bio on some actor instead. You know, to pay the rent.' Robert sounded embarrassed. Was he asking for Richard's approval? 'It's not like I will never write the other book, just that now is not the right time.'

'That's OK.' Richard was surprised to register disappointment in his own voice.

'I have to go,' Robert said. 'See you tomorrow, yes? Maybe talk about it then.'

'Sure,' Richard said. 'See you soon.'

Richard put the receiver back into its cradle.

16

'Can you smoke out here?' Steve said, looking for a sign.

'No idea.' Kate looked around too. It was three in the afternoon, and the beer garden was starting to empty. 'The guy over there is.' She pointed at a lone customer sitting a few tables away reading his newspaper. She saw him flick his ash into a saucer. Steve lit his cigarette.

'Can I take your order?' a waitress asked in perfect English and, not for the first time, Kate felt ashamed of her lack of linguistic ability. She had taken German at school – partly because she wanted to spite her mother, partly because she liked the sound of it – but had never had much talent for it. Fifteen years later she had nothing to show for it.

'I'll have the schnitzel,' Kate said.

'I'll have the same.'

'And to drink?'

'Two beers,' Steve said, and added please in German to be polite. Kate smiled.

'Yes, sir.'

'You know,' Kate said when the waitress had gone, 'a former colleague of mine's friend has to travel a lot, also to Germany, but she never stays overnight here. If she has meetings over two days, she flies home to England to spend the night, then comes back the next day.'

'Why?' Steve asked.

'She said that there were too many angels in Germany.'

'Is she Jewish?'

'Does she have to be Jewish to feel that way?' Kate looked at Steve, annoyed.

'Is she?'

'Yes.' Kate decided that if she had enough money, she too would not spend the night here – if she ever had any reason to come here again. She thought of another anecdote, but decided not to share it with Steve. Paul McCartney never spent a night away from Linda. Or just one, they say. If he did a TV show in Germany, for example, in the evening, he'd fly back to be with her that night rather than return home in the morning, which would have been much more convenient. She wanted to be in love like that. She looked at Steve and wondered whether she'd like him to be the man for whom she'd catch the last flight home, rain or shine. Before she could decide, he announced that he had to take a leak, and Kate decided to defer the decision to another day.

The food and drinks arrived, too quickly for Kate's liking. She was enjoying sitting in the beer garden and observing the people. The solitary customer with the newspaper was still there, and had turned his attention to the sports section.

A few tables down she could see a group of six people having lunch. The two kids, bored, caught her eye and Kate averted her gaze for just a second. When she looked back, she noticed a bee hovering around their table, close to the food, and finally settling on the man's fork. When the man took a bite without looking, the bee flew away, but as soon as he had put his fork back down it landed again, this time on the rim of the man's glass.

Kate looked up at the blue sky. Not a cloud in sight. If there were anywhere in the world where it should rain constantly it should be Germany, she decided. It should rain for as long as it took to cleanse the country of its past, and then just a little bit more. She felt slightly bored, and also homesick.

Whatever she had expected of Germany it wasn't this: this silence, and this friendliness that you could almost touch. She felt as if everyone she saw on the street was a survivor from some horrific plane crash. She could look into people's faces and the faces would tell her: 'Yes, I know what you are thinking. Isn't it horrible what we have done?' Wasn't forgiveness the first step towards healing? At moments like this she was almost ready to do just that. But if she did forgive, would she betray her mother? Kate wished Steve would hurry.

She tried to think back to the day she had seen Steve with the other woman. In retrospect there was no reason to be suspicious; it was she who had jumped to the wrong conclusion and the friendly kiss on the cheek she had seen at a distance meant nothing. Kate almost wished for that irrational jealousy to re-emerge so she could analyse it again and feel it in more detail. Maybe she and Steve should have a fight and make up.

Kate looked for the bee again. It had disappeared; it must either have flown off or fallen into the man's glass. Kate saw him take a sip. He put the glass back down again, and Kate waited for some sort of reaction in his face. Had he swallowed it? But the man seemed happy enough. He smiled, listening to his companion.

'What's up?' Steve asked as he sat down again.

'Nothing.' Kate looked away. 'What took so long?'

'I was only gone a minute.' Steve started on his food, but Kate didn't feel much like eating. He seemed to have been gone for ages.

'I was just thinking,' she said, turning to him.

'Thinking what?' Steve asked again.

'Have you ever done it?' she asked. 'You know, with a prostitute?'

Steve hesitated. 'No.' He cut into his schnitzel. Kate looked at him: if he was flustered he wasn't showing it. Maybe he was lying, but she had seen him at the peep-show and could hardly imagine him going much further.

'Are you sure?' she persisted, and he glanced up at her.

'I think that's the kind of thing I'd remember,' he joked. Kate decided that he was telling the truth.

'Haven't you ever thought about it?'

'Not much.'

Kate shrugged. 'I think I would've.'

'You?'

'Why not? If I were a man.' Kate was sure she would have, given the opportunity. But it was different for women. Women just weren't allowed such luxuries, she thought, looking at Steve and contemplating envying him. 'If you want sex,' she continued, 'and there isn't anybody around you know you can have sex with, why don't you just go and have sex with a prostitute? Do what you have to do.'

'I don't think it's as easy as all that.' Steve said.

She had embarrassed him, she thought. But she hadn't finished yet.

'But *why* wouldn't you?' she insisted. She realised that she had forgotten to keep a track on the man with the bee. When she looked towards his table, the man and his companions had gone, their meals and drinks left behind half finished. Maybe he had been taken to hospital, but she assumed that there would have been some commotion if he had.

'It doesn't seem right,' Steve said.

'What doesn't seem right?' For a moment Kate had forgotten what they were talking about. She was still searching the deserted table for clues as to what had happened to the man. Then she turned back to Steve and looked directly at him.

'I think you take sex *far* too seriously,' she said.

Steve looked at his watch, even though they hadn't anywhere specific to be.

'I want you to do something for me,' Kate said as she took a leisurely sip of her drink.

'What?'

'Promise me first that you will.'

'What is this, primary school?' Steve complained.

'I'm serious.'

'All right,' Steve capitulated, 'I will.' He looked at her attentively.

'I'll tell you later.' Kate finished her beer. 'Your turn to pay,' she said before he could say anything more. She stood up and began to walk to the exit. He took a large sip of his beer, spilling some of it, and followed her.

17

'Let's see what you've got,' Tony said.

The children had assembled in the boys' room just before dark as had been arranged. Jeff, smiling at Tony, then at Sam, removed something from under his jumper. It was a large, juicy steak.

'Steak? You got it a fucking steak?' Tony said. 'You're crazy.'

'But you said get something to eat.' Jeff was disappointed.

'Sure. But not a steak. Not a *fucking* steak.'

'It's OK. It will eat the steak,' Sam said, then immediately felt stupid.

'Of course it will eat the *fucking steak*. But that's dinner,' Tony said. 'I thought he'd get some dog food.'

'Like what?' Sam asked. 'Like where from?'

'I don't know. Like, like . . . ' Tony said. 'I don't know. Something. Not steak.'

'Do you want me to take it back?' Jeff asked.

Sam examined the steak. It had suffered from being under Jeff's jumper. There was no way they could restore it to its original condition. 'We can't take it back now.'

'We'd better go.' Sam looked at her watch. 'We have to

be back in time for bed.'

'Fucking steak,' Tony grumbled. He got up, glancing angrily at Jeff, who was close to tears. 'Don't be such a sissy. Let's go.'

'But it's dark.'

'What, you're afraid of the dark too?' Tony asked.

'No, I'm not. I just thought . . .'

'Yeah?'

'Nothing.'

'We'll borrow the power cut torch from the landing,' said Sam, offering a comforting smile to Jeff.

'We might as well take this, too,' Tony said, and pulled out a torch from under his bed. 'Steak! That dog is in for a treat.'

The torches searched the confines of the electric cage until the beams came to rest on the dog. In the harsh spotlight it looked even more vicious than during the day. Sam really wanted to turn back but she knew that there was no point. Better get it over with as quickly as possible, she thought.

Tony cut off a piece of steak with the Swiss Army knife Dad had given him for his last birthday. Mum had said he was too young for it, and Sam knew how right she was, but now it came in handy.

Tony tried to toss the piece of meat over the fence, but he didn't throw it high enough and it ricocheted back on to the ground next to his feet.

'Shit,' he said. 'Give me some light.' He searched the ground for the meat and finally found it. The second throw made it over the fence, a few yards away from its target, but maybe the dog was too sick or too stupid to get it.

'Come on, it's right next to you,' Jeff said excitedly, but Tony was already preparing the second piece. This time it landed right in front of the dog's nose. It leaped forward.

'Bingo!' Tony shouted, as the dog devoured the piece of meat.

'It must be hungry,' Sam said.

'Of course it's hungry, stupid,' Tony said, and prepared the next piece.

'Whose dog is it?' Jeff asked.

'How should I know?' Tony said, hurling the third piece over the fence. It hit its target again and the dog ate it hungrily. 'See how hungry it is? We have to get it out of there, otherwise it's going to die.'

'I don't want it to die,' Jeff said. 'I'm sure it's a nice dog.'

Sam thought it looked nothing of the sort. 'It doesn't look like a nice dog,' she said.

'It's just a little pissed off,' Tony said. 'Wouldn't you be?'

'I suppose so.'

'Let me throw some, too!' Jeff shouted, but Tony ignored him.

'We have to cut a hole in the fence and get the dog out.'

'That's dangerous,' Sam said.

'Of course it's dangerous. It might bite us or something,' Tony said. He was cutting up all the rest of the meat. 'But we've got to help it. It's our duty.'

'Remember what Mum said,' Sam said.

'What does she know?' Tony mimicked Francesca. 'Stay away, it's dangerous.'

'She's a grown-up.'

'So?'

'So, she knows what to do sometimes.'

'You don't really fall for that bullshit?'

'It's not bullshit,' Sam said, but maybe he had a point. What made the adults so wise anyway? After all, they were just grown-up kids.

'Tony! Please,' Jeff pleaded.

'What?'

'Let me throw some, too.'

'Why didn't you say so?'

Tony gave Jeff the last piece of meat. Jeff smiled and took aim. Sam realised that he was standing much too close to the fence. True enough, the steak hit the fence and fell back down.

'I need some light,' Jeff said.

'Come on, let's go before they start to miss us!' Tony said, and disappeared through the bushes, the beam of his torch instantly lost from view.

Sam looked back nervously at Jeff, who was searching for the last piece of meat.

'Leave it.' She didn't feel comfortable being here after dark. She didn't know how long it would take for their absence to be noticed; they had all pretended to be doing their own thing.

'Leave it!' she shouted angrily, but Jeff carried on looking.

'Wait for me.' Jeff found the meat and hastily picked it up. He aimed it higher than before and threw it. It landed in the no man's land between the first and second fences but the dog could obviously see it. Having gained some strength, the dog started to bite the fence. Its teeth were twisting the wire mesh, and Sam was no longer convinced that it couldn't escape on its own.

'Let's get out of here,' Sam shouted, and made her way back through the bushes, turning to train the torchlight on Jeff's path behind her every so often. The dog barked weakly but angrily as Sam and Jeff reached the path, got on their bikes and rushed to catch up with Tony.

In the cold of the night Sam could see her breath clearly but, apart from the pool of light in front of her from her bicycle lamp, it was pitch-black. Tony must already be halfway to the house, she thought, while Jeff was still a considerable distance behind her, although she didn't dare look back in case the dog had bitten its way free and was already following them.

Sam was glad to see the lights of the house as she cleared the forest, and as she allowed herself to slow down she could hear Jeff cycling behind her. Immediately she felt guilty. She slowed down more and as she reached the gate she stopped. Jeff looked ashen-faced when he finally caught up with her. His shoelaces were undone, and Sam counted both herself and him lucky that he hadn't come off the bike again.

'It's OK,' she said, trying to calm their fears. 'He can't get out of there.' She got off her bike and tied Jeff's laces.

'Then why did you cycle so fast?'

'It looks like rain.' Sam looked up in the moonlit sky. There were indeed a few dark clouds, but she hadn't noticed them before.

'I was really frightened.'

'Don't be frightened. It's just a silly old dog,' Sam said. 'It's too weak to do anything. Too weak to bite its way out of there, anyhow.'

'Then we have to do something,' Jeff said. 'Tony says we have to cut it free.'

'Maybe. We can think about it tomorrow.' Sam got on her bike again. 'We'll have to have a secret meeting about it.'

'Am I invited?'

'Of course you are.'

Jeff's eyes lit up. He had never been invited to a secret meeting before.

Sam would have to break the news of Jeff's presence to Tony. He wouldn't be happy. But, anyway, they might need Jeff if they wanted to free the dog. 'Come on, let's go.'

Sam opened the gate and let Jeff pass through it first. She took a cautious glance back towards the forest. Its black mass looked at her menacingly and dared her to return.

18

'I think you should do it.'

'Do what?' Kate and Steve were walking in the English Garden, a massive park in the centre of Munich. English, Kate had read in Steve's guidebook, because it was not regimented. Looking at the trees and bushes, allowed to grow informally as they wanted to, she felt proud at the chaos, even though she supposed that to have an English garden there also had to be some rules.

'Have sex with a prostitute.'

Steve stopped in his tracks and his mouth dropped open. Just like in a cartoon, Kate thought, and for a moment she was amazed at the power she had over him.

'You are kidding, right?' He looked around, as if to see whether there were any spectators, or at least a team from *Candid Camera*.

'I have never been more serious,' Kate said. She looked into Steve's eyes to see if she could gauge his exact feelings for her now, but all she could see was that he was nonplussed. She was, however, pleased to have his full attention.

Only once she had said it did Kate know that this was

what she really wanted. Could she feel a hint of jealousy already, or was it just nerves about whether she had made the right decision? She wanted to feel about him as she had the first time after she had met him, but on her own terms this time, and she really had to be sure Steve was with her not to have sex but to make love, that he wanted her because of everything she was. Not just because she was a woman, and available, but because she was Kate. Steve's shock now turned into puzzled bemusement.

'You can't be serious,' he said, but Kate could see that he knew full well she was.

'And why shouldn't I be?'

'It's just not what people ask from their partner,' Steve said.

Partner. Kate decided to let that one slip.

'I'm not people. Anyway, how do you know?'

'No one has ever asked me before.'

'And you've had so many lovers?'

'No.'

'How many?'

'Is this really necessary?'

'Yes.'

'Ten, twelve.'

'What, you lost count?'

'Nine.'

They continued to walk in silence for a while. Kate glanced at him, but he was staring into space. She half dreaded him asking how many people she had slept with, but he didn't. He must be afraid of the answer.

'There's no way,' Steve said as they walked towards the gates of the garden.

'Suit yourself,' Kate said. 'It was only a suggestion.'

'Come on, tell me what's wrong.' Steve took her hand and stopped her from walking. It was late afternoon, and the shadows were getting longer. Soon the warmth of the sun would be gone.

'Nothing's wrong. I've got a headache. 'Can we get a cab?' she asked, but before he had a chance to answer she had already hailed one. She got in and slammed the door shut. For a moment Steve thought she might be driven off without him, but the driver waited until he had got in the other side.

They sat in silence. The taxi driver looked at Steve in the mirror. Taxi drivers must gauge the mood of their clients immediately, he thought, as they drove through an area that to Steve was increasingly unfamiliar. He hoped that he had given the right instructions, and supposed he should confirm.

'You know what you're asking from me?' he said to Kate, instead, but she could sense that he had got over the shock.

'Yes.'

'But why?'

'I just want to make sure that you're not into me just for the sex,' she said.

'But I'm not.' Steve lowered his voice, wondering if the taxi driver could understand what they were saying. He would be the first German who didn't.

'Then prove it.'

'And what's the point?'

'It will show you that you can have sex any time, anywhere. That you don't need me for it. So that's when you come to me, when you need me, and not just my body.'

'And if I don't?'

'Then we *still* have a future, don't you see?' Kate smiled. 'I'm not forcing you to do it, I just think it would benefit us both.'

'You're crazy, you know?' Steve laughed despite himself.

'I'm not sure. Sometimes I think I'm too sensible.' Kate put her hand on his knee and started to caress it. 'Admit it, you quite like the idea?'

'I do not!'

'Not even a tiny bit?'

'Hands off,' Steve said, trying to sound as uninterested as he could. But when she removed her hand, the place on his leg felt cold, and he put her hand back again. She moved it up towards his crotch. He leaned over and kissed her.

'If you can do this, I'll know that I can ask anything from you. That you'll always be there for me.'

'You *can* ask anything from me.'

'I want you to always be there for me.'

Steve noticed familiar buildings and was relieved that they were headed in the right direction. 'You're really serious, aren't you?'

'I am.'

'I love you, you know,' Steve said.

'I love you, too.' Kate noticed that this was the first time they had said that without jokes, and while not making love. It made her feel good, and she looked forward to hearing it again and again.

19

The blanket felt too warm, but for a secret meeting one had to get under a blanket, switch off the lights and use torches. Sam, Tony and Jeff had gathered under the blanket in the wardrobe of the boys' room. Whoever's turn it was to speak had to hold a torch up to their face. That was to make sure that only one person could speak at a time, although it usually meant that it was Tony who got to say most, as he would only yield the torch to anyone else when he had said what he wanted, and would grab it back whenever he pleased.

'We have to do it. It's our responsibility,' Tony said, and handed the torch to Sam.

'I agree. We have to do something.' Sam handed the torch to Jeff. It was his first time, and he grinned.

'Say something,' Tony said, without the torch.

'I second the emotion,' Jeff said, and Sam and Tony burst out laughing.

'I second the *motion*, stupid,' Tony said, again without the torch.

Sam took the torch. 'But it's dangerous.'

'Of course it's dangerous. That's why we have to have a

plan,' Tony said, getting the torch halfway through speaking the words. 'The important decision to make is how we're going to get it out.'

'How *are* we going to get it?' Sam asked.

'We can cut the wire or . . .' Tony paused.

'Or what?'

'We can dig under the fence.' Tony smiled. 'We can get the tools from Granddad's shed. He won't know they're missing.'

'And the dog is just going to come out?' Sam asked.

'I don't think so,' Tony said. 'It doesn't look like it will ever want to move.'

'So?'

'So we have to tease it out. Lay a trail of food or something. Like in *Snow White*.'

'*Hansel and Gretel*,' Jeff said.

'It's just a stupid dog, why don't we just leave it?' Sam suggested, but Tony wasn't listening.

'It's not stupid!' Jeff said.

'Use the torch,' Tony said angrily, handing it to him.

'It's not stupid. I think we should save it.'

Tony took the torch back. 'One of us has to get it,' he said, looking at Jeff and Sam, and then at Jeff again. 'We'd have to dig deep enough for you to fit under it.'

'Why Jeff?' Sam asked.

'He's the smallest. We won't have to dig too deep.'

'We can cut the fence. It's easy to cut a hole big enough for you to get through,' Sam suggested.

'Me?'

'You should go,' Sam said to Tony. 'It is your idea. And it's too dangerous for Jeff.'

'If we cut a hole in the fence,' Tony said, 'they're going to find out.'

'What if we dig a hole?' Sam said. 'They're going to

discover that, too, aren't they?'

'We can fill that back in, stupid.'

Sam was annoyed with herself.

'I don't mind doing it,' Jeff said.

'See,' Tony said to Sam. 'It makes sense that Jeff goes. And it's not that dangerous.'

'And what if the dog attacks him? What if there is electricity in there?'

'What if? What if? What if a meteor crashes down and kills us all? The dog won't attack him, and there can't be that much electricity in there, otherwise the dog wouldn't still be alive. It's not dangerous,' Tony said again, and added, as if to convince himself, 'Piece of cake.'

'No, it isn't,' Sam said.

'Are you in or not?' Tony said, and Jeff and Tony looked at Sam.

'Sure I am,' Sam said. She'd have to be careful. 'If we draw straws for who is going to do it,' she added quickly. 'Get the dog out.'

'OK, we'll draw straws,' Tony conceded. Sam thought she could just make out the glimmer of a smile falling across his face.

'When?' Sam asked.

'This afternoon. Before dinner,' Tony said. 'We can get yesterday's leftovers to make it come out.'

'Can't we wait until tomorrow?' Sam asked.

'We can't wait. The dog is already half dead. We'll get the tools and get him. OK?'

'OK.'

'OK.'

'Let's draw straws.' Tony took his matchbox out of his back pocket and retrieved three matches. Sam watched carefully as he broke one in half.

'Let me do the draw,' she offered.

'Why?'

'Why not?'

Sam was surprised when Tony agreed and handed her the matches. She checked them, then mixed them up with her hand behind her back. She decided that if Jeff drew the short straw, she would volunteer in his place. They would have to dig the hole a little deeper, but she would volunteer to do that, too. And volunteer to fill it back in afterwards.

She stretched out the hand with the straws in it.

'Who goes first?' Jeff asked excitedly.

'Be my guest,' Tony said.

Jeff pulled a match. It was long, and Sam could make out disappointment in his face. Tony looked a little nervous.

'Now you,' Sam said.

Tony looked carefully at the two remaining matches, touched one and then decided on the other. He pulled it out of Sam's hand. It was the short one.

Sam felt relief. It couldn't have worked out any better.

Tony took the torch again. 'It's dangerous, but I know that I can rely on you to help me,' he said, playing the part of the martyr well.

'I'm not chicken,' Sam said.

'Me neither.'

'But we have to be careful.'

'Swear we'll stick together on this,' Tony said, looking around the circle. 'Swear.'

'I swear.'

'Me too,' Jeff said.

Tony declared the meeting closed and switched off the torch.

20

Steve walked along the main street of the red-light district, not far from the peep-show they had visited. Kate followed ten yards behind him, like a bad detective shadowing his every move. Not for the first time, he stopped and turned to her and waved her away.

He turned into a side street. When he realised that Kate was still following him, he turned and mouthed, 'Go away,' which finally did the trick. She took a quick glance around and indicated a café on the other side of the street, and Steve nodded. He watched her cross over and made sure she disappeared through the door. He turned and was surprised to find himself looking straight into the face of a young woman. She was almost as tall as he was.

'*Willst du eine Frau?*' she asked him. He could smell her perfume. She didn't smell bad.

'*Nein, danke.*'

She didn't look too bad, either, Steve thought, as she walked on, but he would need more time. On the other side of the street he saw Kate take a window seat in the café and order something, all the time keeping an eye on him. He waved at her, trying to discourage her, but she only waved back. Was it all just one big joke to her?

Turning again, he felt distinctly uncomfortable. The café hadn't been such a good idea. It was the perfect vantage point from which to observe him. From her seat Kate pointed at a house that had several windows with red lights on the second floor. Steve sighed. He might as well.

He entered, and was relieved that Kate could no longer see him. He walked up the stairs of the apartment building. On the second floor, he stopped at a door that had a notice: '*Modell*'. He took a deep breath. He was about to grasp the door handle when the door opened and a middle-aged man emerged. He smiled at Steve, and Steve half expected him to wink. The man held the door open for him.

'Third floor, *drei Stock*?' Steve asked and the man pointed at a sign that clearly indicated this was the second floor.

The man let the door fall back into the lock. Steve walked further up the stairs, and as soon as he was out of the man's sight he stopped. When he was sure that the man had gone he walked down the stairs again, passed the door on the second floor without even glancing at it, and left the building.

When he emerged from the front door, he felt like going to tell Kate that he couldn't go through with it when he saw her reading a newspaper in the café. She was really taking the whole thing lightly, he thought, walking back up the street. Or was she just expecting him to fail?

Not for the first time since the early days of their relationship, Steve was worried about losing her, and he was all the more determined to find a woman who wasn't Kate but with whom he could imagine having sex. She was right, what difference did it make?

21

Kate clung on tightly to the newspaper. She had grabbed it as soon as she had sat down, for something to hold on to, and she hadn't even registered that it was in German. As she saw Steve on the street opposite the café she waved him on, more to stop having to observe him than as a call to action. She couldn't face the coffee she had ordered, delivered in no time by the sole waitress. She had found a seat by the window, but would have preferred one at the back, staring at the wall, until it was all over. She looked out of the window. Steve had disappeared.

She tried to catch the waitress's eye to order something stronger, but she was busy chatting with a man, her back turned to Kate. All the tables were busy. It must be almost dinnertime now. Kate wondered how hectic dinner at home would be. It was Sunday and everyone would be there. Everyone apart from her. What were the children up to? She missed them to bits.

This holiday had been a bad idea. Steve and she should have gone somewhere warm and just concentrated on each other, instead of throwing Germany into the mix. It was too early. She had been so certain of everything; only now, on her own, with time to think, she was not so sure about anything any more.

She wondered how long Steve would take. She thought that if he had decided not to go through with it, he'd be back by now. Maybe he couldn't find anyone suitable, but from the women she had seen in the area, she was sure that someone would appeal to Steve enough. Would it take half an hour? Ten minutes? The feeling of jealousy she had sought to evoke didn't materialise; instead she felt sick to her stomach.

Kate noticed a mother and her daughter at the table opposite her. Without much enthusiasm the girl was eating an ice cream with a long spoon out of beaker. She must be about twelve, Kate guessed, and she was the spitting image of her mother, except for the cigarette her mum was puffing. The child seemed to be in trouble, and the mother was talking to her intently.

As Kate contemplated the houses opposite through the light traffic, Kate was reminded of a friend who had suggested that cars had killed more people than Hitler had killed Jews. Did intention matter? What if a brilliant scientist invented a teleportation machine, which malfunctioned often enough to cause the same number of casualties that cars produced today? Would it be passed by the relevant authorities? Another friend had told her that formula milk companies' aggressive marketing of infant formula in poor countries, where access to clean drinking water was scarce, cost the lives of one newborn every thirty seconds. And here she sat while she worried about her boyfriend having meaningless sex with a woman he had never met.

The girl's mother at the table opposite was still talking at her, but her daughter seemed to be more interested in looking at Kate. What is so interesting about me? Kate wondered, and briefly felt flattered, then realised she was crying. She grabbed a tissue from her bag.

Sitting in this random café in Germany, Kate suddenly understood the new feeling she was experiencing: she felt complicit. How was she different from the German family who did not know what had happened to their friendly neighbours who had just disappeared from one day to the next? Do I not know what is happening to others? Kate thought. What is my excuse? How did the German expression go? *Was ich nicht weiß, macht mich nicht heiß* – the only German she had learned from her mother, a history lesson rather than a language lesson. 'What I do not know, does not make me hot.' The excuse used to be, 'I did not know'; today, in the age of the Internet and rolling news it has become 'information overload'.

Kate decided that the only thing that separates us from those who watched in silence while the Nazis killed millions, is that while most of those are no longer alive, we are. If Germany was a warning from history, it seemed to have had the opposite effect. The Holocaust had succeeded in compartmentalising evil. It had made bystanders feel that they were not complicit. But is it not within ourselves where the true horror lies?

'*Hast du das verstanden?*' the mother at the table opposite snapped at her daughter. The child was still looking at Kate, but her mother demanded the child's full attention and, reaching out for her chin, turned her head in her direction, almost as if she were a puppet. '*Verstanden?*' the mother repeated. She let go of her, and the child nodded. Had she understood? Kate wondered. Or was she just nodding to get out of trouble?

The mother looked at Kate, but evidently didn't find her as interesting as her daughter did, and turned away. Kate wondered what the argument had been about.

'*Komm, wir gehen.*' The woman finished her drink, lit

another cigarette and prepared to go. The girl finished the last spoonfuls of her ice cream as quickly as she could. The mother got up and grabbed her daughter by the hand. As they left, they had to squeeze past Kate's table and the mother offered a quick '*Entschuldigung*'. Was she apologising for disturbing Kate's chair or for shouting at her daughter in front of her?

When they had gone Kate looked out of the window again, and at the door Steve had disappeared through. What had she done?

'Shit,' she said, loud enough for a couple to turn to her. As she got up, she almost knocked over the table and spilled some of her untouched coffee. She looked for the waitress, but she was still chatting to the man. Her boyfriend, Kate assumed, the one who might be a keeper, unlike the one Kate was about to lose.

Kate rummaged through her bag and put a ten-euro bill on the table. Far too much, she knew, but she had to get out of there as quickly as possible. She grabbed her jacket, put her bag over her shoulder and left.

22

Sam could see the disappointment in Tony's face, but as far as she was concerned a heavy load had been lifted off her shoulders. She put the dog food back in her bag. They wouldn't need it now. She had bought it with her pocket money from the local shop, to help guide the dog out through the hole and to freedom. She was still worried that word would get back to Grandma from the owner of the shop, but it was better than stealing more steaks.

'It's dead,' Sam said.

'I can see that,' Tony said.

Now that it could no longer harm them, Sam almost felt sorry for it. Maybe they should have done all of this sooner, she found herself thinking, but quickly dismissed the thought. The dog was dead. Problem solved.

Standing at the fence, they could see the dog lying on the ground, its eyes wide open. Flies were buzzing around it.

'Why is it dead?' Jeff asked, and Sam looked at his tiny fingers gripping the fence. She hoped he wouldn't cry.

'We were too late.' Sam took Jeff's hand. 'It's probably better this way. It probably didn't have anyone it belonged to anyway. Come on. Let's go home.'

Tony looked at Sam, and she tried to look away as quickly as possible, hoping that he wouldn't make out her sense of relief. Another one of his stupid games was finished. And once again it wasn't he who had finished it.

'We can't leave it in there like that,' Jeff said, still standing at the fence.

'What can we do?' Sam asked. 'It's dead.'

'It'll rot,' Tony confirmed, and Sam could see the hint of a smile returning to his face.

'Let's go home.' Sam pulled Jeff a little more forcefully than she would have liked and he let go of the fence. He stumbled a couple of steps in the direction of the bushes, but stopped again. He was still looking at the dog, full of fascination.

Tony, too, seemed to have no intention of going. Suddenly his face lit up. 'He deserves a decent burial.'

'No, let's go home. Please,' Sam pleaded. 'Or let's go to the beach.'

'The beach is boring,' Tony said.

'The beach is *not* boring,' Sam said. 'You haven't broken my record.'

'Who cares about your stupid record?' Tony said. 'I can beat that any time.'

'No, you can't,' Sam said, but she knew that he wouldn't take the bait.

Tony turned to her again. 'Jeff is right,' he said. 'We can't just leave him like that.'

'It's just a stupid dog.' Sam looked at Tony and then at Jeff. She had thought it was over but only now realised how wrong she had been. They were going to do something crazy just to bury a stupid dog.

'Are you going to help us or not?' Tony looked at her challengingly.

'Come on, Jeff,' Sam said again. 'Let's go home and play

inside. We haven't finished playing the tiles game.'

'But what about the dog?' Jeff had returned to the fence and looked at the dead dog.

'The dog is dead,' Sam said. 'No one can help it now. We were too late.'

'We have to bury it,' Jeff aped Tony, and Sam thought he really believed it. 'We can't just leave it there.'

'We have to bury it,' Tony confirmed. Jeff seemed pleased.

'Suit yourself. I'm going,' Sam said.

'You promised,' Tony said.

'I promised to help get the dog out alive. But it's dead.'

'You swore,' Jeff said.

'Well, I'm breaking my promise. The dog is dead.' Sam could hear herself sounding very adult. Tony would hate her for that.

'If you go now, don't come back,' he said.

She could see it would be hopeless trying to get him to give up on the idea. At least the dog was harmless now. It was just the electricity she was worried about. The loose cable was still swaying about dangerously in the wind.

'I don't want to come back to this place anyway. It gives me the creeps.' Sam turned to go.

'Chicken,' Tony said, but his taunt didn't hurt her.

'Yeah, big chicken,' Jeff said, smiling broadly.

'Enormous chicken.' Tony was already starting to unpack the tools.

'I'm going to tell,' Sam said.

'No, you won't.'

'I will, too.'

'If you tell I'll . . .'

'You'll what?'

'I'll think of something,' Tony said, but Sam had already vanished into the bushes, leaving him standing there with the shovel.

23

Kate crossed the street, trying to find a gap in the traffic and walked the few yards up to the entrance she herself had suggested to Steve. She stopped, but the tide of pedestrians made it impossible for her to contemplate her situation for long. She mustered her courage and entered.

She could make out a bad stench coming from a collection of overflowing rubbish bins. It was that smell as much as her desire to stop Steve that made her pull herself together and climb the stairs.

As soon as she had climbed up to the first half-landing she heard footsteps. She quickly realised the slow footfalls where those of an older man, not Steve. A figure approached and she sensed the man looking at her. When she did finally look up at him – out of a remnant of curiosity, perhaps – she saw him avert his eyes.

Having gained a little confidence, she climbed up further, passing the first-floor door, which seemed to be to offices of some sort. She was sure she was already too late. She doubted that a brothel would have a waiting room. She almost laughed. Pick a number and wait your turn. Read a dirty magazine while you wait.

What would she do if she did get there in time? What would she tell him? Sorry, I changed my mind. Let's have a drink and let me tell you why. Kate didn't know why she had changed her mind. What would she tell him if she was too late? She'd have to put on a front again, pretend that she was keen to hear what happened, but that was the last thing she felt like doing now. She'd get over it, but in her own time.

She hastened her pace and climbed the remaining steps as fast as she could without running. She arrived on the second floor and found a single door. The word '*Modell*' made from Letraset on a tired piece of cardboard was the only indication that this was where he might be.

She hesitated, but knew she didn't have any time to lose. She knocked quietly, almost fearful of attracting attention. There was no reply, and she knocked a little louder, but the old wooden door was too heavy to carry much sound. She looked for a bell, but there wasn't one.

She was about to give up when she decided to give it one last try. She pushed the door, and it swung open without so much as a sound. The stone floor of the corridor changed to a linoleum covering beyond the door, and as she entered, her steps rang hollow on it.

Several rooms led off a corridor, and Kate was relieved that the doors were all more or less open. There was no sound. Business must be slow, she thought, or was it too early? She peeked in one of the rooms as discreetly as she could, and it looked almost like a hostel: apart from the bed and a small bedside table there was no other furniture.

'Hello?' she said, but too quietly to have any serious chance of being heard. The apartment seemed to be deserted. She walked to the end of the corridor, wondering whether she was in the right place. This could almost be a family home. She half expected to be arrested for trespassing. She would have to spend the rest of her holiday in jail. That would teach me, she thought.

She saw a kid's bike with stabilisers on it at the end of the corridor, and was about to turn to go when she made out the sound of a soft groan from the back of the apartment. The groan became louder and louder, as a woman seemed to approach orgasm. Kate could feel a tear rise in her eye, and was about to turn when the groan changed to laughter. It wasn't joined by Steve's laughter, or even another man's, but by the laughter of other women.

Kate took a deep breath and decided to investigate. She walked back along the corridor and stepped into the room the noise had come from. It was a kitchen, a long room with a high window at one end. Under the window four women were sitting around a small table, its bright plastic tablecloth the only colour in the grey kitchen.

One of them, a tired-looking blonde in her late thirties, looked up at Kate. '*Wir haben Pause,*' she said, not at all put out by this strange woman turning up in her apartment.

'Sorry to disturb you,' Kate said. 'Is this the right place?' She looked around for any evidence that the place was actually a brothel, but was not sure what she was expecting to find. The women were all wearing cheap casual clothes and could have been housewives, even cleaners. 'I'm looking for a man,' she said.

'*Wir haben nur Frauen,*' another of the women replied and everyone laughed. Kate could piece the meaning together: we only have women.

But she was undeterred. 'He's about this tall, dark hair, around thirty, brown eyes, wearing a grey shirt and black jeans. Have you seen him?' She left the hand with which she had indicated Steve's height in the air as if this would conjure up an accurate image of him, but it suddenly occurred to her that the women might not speak English. '*Sprechen sie Englisch?*'

'I see one of those every half an hour, ten hours a day,' the first woman said in English, looking at one of her colleagues. 'The other half wear suits and are around fifty.' This time their laughter sounded more bitter than amused.

'He's my boyfriend,' Kate offered, and at first she thought they'd start laughing again. However, one of the women, she must have been the youngest, Kate thought, took pity on her.

'When would he have been here?' she said, with only a faint hint of an accent in her voice. She sounded smart – a student making ends meet? Kate wondered.

'Within the last ten minutes,' Kate said. She knew she was in the wrong place and that while she was playing detective here, Steve was having it off with a stranger a couple of doors along. Up a different seedy staircase.

'There hasn't been anyone here for an hour,' the young woman confirmed. 'We're having a break. It's Marion's birthday.' It was only now that Kate noticed the birthday cake on the table. Chocolate cake and wine, not her favourite combination. She felt sick.

'Happy birthday,' Kate said, absent-mindedly.

'Thank you.'

'I have to go,' she said, and turned to leave. She couldn't bear being in that place a second longer than she needed to be. Her brisk walk turned into a sprint, and she found herself running down the stairs two at a time, desperate to be out in the open. Halfway down the stairs she stopped breathing, and she allowed herself a fresh intake of air only once she was outside on the street again.

24

Steve had decided to look for the woman he had spoken to earlier. He scanned the street, but she was gone. Was she with a client? He was surprised when he felt a twinge of jealousy. Now that he had decided it was she he wanted, he walked up and down the street impatiently.

He was pleased when he saw her emerging from round a street corner, putting out a cigarette. He started walking up to her quickly, but as he approached, he slowed his steps. He almost changed his mind as she came closer, but she had seen him. There seemed to be no kindness in her eyes, but why should there be? He was about to walk away again but couldn't face snubbing her a second time. He wondered what to say.

'*Hast dich anders entschieden?*' the prostitute asked, before he could think of something to say.

'How much?' Steve tried to sound businesslike but knew he was failing miserably. He felt more like a teenager trying to lose his virginity than a man trying to humour his girlfriend.

'One hundred euros.' She had switched to English without a hint of hesitation.

'OK.' Steve had had no idea how much it would cost. He had three hundred euros ready in his pocket, a sum that Kate and he had decided should be sufficient.

'Come on,' the prostitute said. Steve hesitated. 'Follow me.' She walked into a dark doorway, and for a moment Steve thought they would do it right there. He wished he knew her name but didn't think it was a good time to ask.

He was relieved when she opened the door and began to walk up the stairs. The house was clean, and the nameplates on the door looked like those of any other house. Do people live here? he wondered. He watched the prostitute climbing the stairs. How often had she done this trip? Five, ten times a day? More often? From behind, she could almost be Kate, he thought, with her short brown hair, her tight jeans, her determined walk. Is that why I picked her?

The stairs seemed endless, but that suited him just fine. Now that he had decided to go through with it, he was not that nervous any more, but wanted to relish the experience. He thought that Kate would ask about every little detail later, and their erotically charged conversation would inevitably result in their making love that night. He looked around, trying to take in as many details as possible.

'This is it,' she said. They had climbed the stairs all the way up to the top floor. Steve was a little out of breath but tried not to show it.

The woman unlocked the only door, and pushed it open. The door revealed a large apartment, right under the roof of the house. As he walked along the corridor, he could see a young child on the floor of one of the rooms, watching television. The prostitute looked at Steve angrily and shut the door. She led him to a small room at the back. 'I'll be right back.'

Steve was left alone. There was only a single bed and

a chair in the room, nothing on the walls, no light apart from a bare light bulb on the ceiling. This must be the least erotic room he had ever seen. He wondered what to do. There was only one high window in the room, and he tried to look out, but he could make out only the sky. It hadn't turned dark yet. He thought of Kate waiting in the café, reading her newspaper. Was she really as nonchalant about this as she pretended to be?

He heard the muffled voice of a man next door. Her pimp? Maybe they were planning to mug him? What was keeping her? He had almost begun to think that the prostitute had forgotten about him, when she came back into the room.

'You are still dressed?' she asked.

'Sorry.'

'The money,' she said.

Steve fumbled in his pocket and got out two fifty-euro bills. 'Here.' He handed her the money.

'For an extra fifty I'll take my top off.'

Steve looked at her, puzzled. 'No, thank you,' he said.

She shrugged, an exaggerated gesture, and put the money into her pocket.

The woman sat down on the bed, took her shoes off and began to unbutton her jeans. She looked bored.

'What's your name?' Steve asked.

'Julia.' She said it quickly and with enough indifference for Steve to assume that it must be her real name.

'I'm Steve,' he said.

'Get undressed. I don't have all day,' Julia said.

Steve started to unbutton his shirt.

25

Sam was walking up the path towards the house, feeling lonely. She was also feeling a little guilty about having left Jeff there. She supposed that with the dog dead it would be a pretty harmless thing to do, to go in and fetch it, that is, if they were careful with the electricity. Tony had electrocuted himself trying to change the plug of a broken CD player before, but Jeff was still pretty fearless as far as electricity was concerned. What if Tony really got Jeff to do the whole job?

Even if it all went well and was boring, Tony would be talking about this for weeks, if not months. Talking about how she chickened out and how they had buried the dog. And maybe he was right. Who was she to say that the dog should just lie there and rot? Dogs had rights, too.

She thought about going back and helping out, but it would be too late to do it without losing face. But she should go and make sure that Tony didn't mess up. Jeff didn't know any better than to do what people told him. She could think of an excuse and hope that Tony wouldn't pick up on it. But she could already see the house peeking through the trees, and the thought of going all the way back didn't appeal to her. She'd play some games on her own, or read something, and wait for them to return, she thought, as she approached the front door.

'So young and so deep in thought.'

Sam hadn't noticed Richard walking towards her. He must be going on one of his strolls. Sam had no idea where he went, and she half hoped that he would take her along this time. That would annoy Tony. If it was boring she could always make something up. Something exciting that made Tony really envious.

'Hi, Granddad,' Sam said.

'What are you thinking about?'

'Nothing.'

For a brief moment Sam thought about telling him everything. About the electricity substation, how they had found the dog, and about the mystery of the missing steak. And explain that now the dog was dead. And how Tony was going to take it out of there and give it a decent burial. Endangering Jeff's life, but probably not.

It's probably nothing, Sam would reassure her granddad. But maybe we had better check it out. And Granddad would go with her to the transformer and save Jeff, just before he got fried like bacon. And Sam would be the hero, and even Tony would thank her. Well, he wouldn't actually say so, but she guessed that from that moment on he would treat her with a little more respect. Listen to what she had to say.

But looking at Granddad she knew she wouldn't say a word. She didn't want to tell on Tony. She could just about bear being called a chicken, but she wasn't going to be called a snitch.

'It's always nothing.' Richard had bent down to her level. She remembered when he would have to go down on his knees but now he had to stoop only a little.

'Granddad?' she asked.

'Yes?' He looked at her as if there might be something hidden in her face, but she didn't think he could find it.

'Nothing.'

Richard gazed steadily at her.

'Nothing?'

'You know, kids' stuff.'

Richard smiled, turned to go, but hesitated. 'You will look after yourself, won't you, my little princess?'

'Sure thing, Granddad,' Sam said.

'Sure thing?' Richard smiled. 'Careful, or you'll turn into an American, like me.'

Sam looked up at the house and at the window of Richard's study and had an idea. It would be ages before Tony and Jeff got back, and Granddad probably would be gone for a good while. Grandma would be busy doing her painting, and Mum and Dad had gone back to London after lunch.

Sam went inside. She took off her jacket and shoes as quickly as possible and rushed up the stairs into Granddad's study. As she pushed open the door, she realised that this was maybe the first time she had been there alone. She stood in the middle of the room and looked out of the window, just to make sure her granddad wasn't heading back to get something he had forgotten.

She waited a long minute until she decided it was safe. She crawled under Richard's desk and pushed the drawer open, then crawled out again to retrieve the packet with the videotape she had seen him look at the other day. The tape was unmarked, and Sam shrugged exaggeratedly, as if this would confirm to an invisible onlooker that it would be legitimate to watch it without her granddad's permission.

Sam switched on the TV and put the videotape into the player that rested on top of it. Before she could make a final decision about whether to watch it – maybe this wasn't something a little kid should see – the tape started to run automatically, and a black-and-white picture appeared on the screen.

26

Sam sat down on the floor, half trying to keep an eye on the door, but the film was demanding her full attention. It was a bad copy: scratches ran through it, and the sound was muffled. Whatever it was took place at Yale University, and a man in a white lab technician's coat was shaking the hands of two men who had turned up in his offices. Sam had to strain to make out what the man in white was saying in a matter-of-fact American accent to the men in suits. It looked as if they had turned up for job interviews.

'There's a seat right here,' the scientist said. 'Now, both of you have been paid. Why don't you sit down right here?' The two men sat down next to each other on two chairs, just as if they were in a doctor's waiting room. 'Let me say that this fee is for showing up at the lab. From this point on, no matter what happens, the money is yours. I should like to tell both of you a little about the memory project.'

This must have been years ago. What has it to do with Granddad? Sam wondered, but even before she could finish the thought she knew. The man sitting closest to the scientist was Richard. Even though he must have been half his current age in this film, she could still recognise his features. As ever, he looked as though he didn't want to be there. Sam smiled. He was famous, he was in a film! Why would he want to hide it from us? she asked herself, resting her chin in her hands.

The scientist continued, 'One theory is that people learn things correctly whenever they get punished making a mistake. A common application of this theory would be when parents spank a child when he does something wrong. But, actually, we know very little about the effect of punishment on learning, because almost no truly scientific studies have been made of it in human beings.

'So what we are doing with this project is bringing together a number of adults with different occupations and ages and asking some of them to be teachers and some to be learners. We wanted to find out just what effect different people have on each other as teachers and learners, and also what effect punishment will have on learning in this situation.

'Therefore, I'm going to ask one of you to be the teacher here this afternoon; the other will be the learner. And the way we usually decide is to let you draw from these two pieces of paper on which I have written the two positions. If this is agreeable to you both, please take one of the pieces of paper.'

They each took one. Just like picking straws, Sam thought.

'Can you look at them and tell me which of you is which, please?' Richard had taken the one with 'Teacher' on it, and Sam giggled. She couldn't really see him as the teacher type, even though he knew a lot of things. This was going to be fun.

'The next thing we'll have to do,' the man in the white coat continued, 'is set the learner up so he can get some sort of punishment. Learner, would you step out here with me, please?'

The other man got up and looked at a machine that was standing on the desk. It had lots of switches in a row, all marked with voltages and notices reading from 'SLIGHT SHOCK' to 'DANGER: SEVERE SHOCK'. This certainly looks dangerous, Sam thought, especially the last few switches, which were just marked 'XXX'. I have to make sure that Tony doesn't get hold of this tape, she decided; he'd love it.

The man who was going to be the learner followed the scientist into the next room. 'Do you want to step in here and take a seat, please?' the scientist said. 'You can leave your coat on the back of that chair.' The learner took off his jacket. 'Thank you very much. That's fine.

'Pull yourself right up to the counter, please.' As the learner sat down, the scientist turned to Richard, who was still waiting outside the room. 'You may look on if you like while we get set up in here.' Richard entered the room and watched as the learner got into position. Sam could see a few wires on the desk in front of him. Were they going to hook him up to the electricity generator?

'Would you roll up your right sleeve, please?' the scientist asked the learner. 'What I am going to do is to strap your arms down to avoid any excessive movement on your part during the experiment.' He strapped one of the learner's arms to the arm of the chair. 'Is that too tight?'

'That's fine,' the learner said.

He strapped down the second one and began to attach one of the wires to each of the learner's arms. 'This electrode is connected to the shock generator in the next room,' the scientist explained, and took a tube of what looked like glue. 'And this electrode paste is to provide a good contact and to avoid any blister or burn,' he explained.

'And now let me explain to you, learner, exactly what's going to happen and what you're supposed to do. The teacher will read a list of word-pairs to you like these, Blue – Girl, Nice – Day, Fat – Neck, and so forth. You want to try and remember each pair, for the next time through the teacher will read only the first word, the first half of the pair.'

Granddad was listening attentively to the scientist. It was just like being at school, Sam thought and giggled.

'For example, he will say Blue, and then he'll read four other words such as Boy, Girl, Grass, Hat. Now, our job is to remember which one of these four other words was originally paired with Blue and to indicate your answer by pressing one of these four switches. Now, can you reach those all right?'

The learner flicked the switches in front of him one by one and the scientist seemed happy.

'That's fine. If the first word I just read, Boy, had been paired with Blue, you'd press the first switch, and this will indicate to the teacher that you thought it was the first word. If you thought it had been the second word, Girl, you'd press the second switch. So forth for the third word, the third switch, the fourth word, the fourth switch.

'Now, if you get it correct, fine. If you make an error, however, you will punished with an electric shock, so of course it is to your advantage that you learn all the word-pairs as quickly as possible.'

Sam thought that Jeff would have been good at this, and imagined him sitting in the other room, taking the scientist by surprise. The scientist led Richard into the other room with the electricity generator in it.

'This machine generates electric shocks,' he explained to Richard, 'and if you press one of these switches all the way down, the learner gets a shock. When you release it the shock stops, you see. Like that.' The scientist flicked a switch. 'The switch will remain in its middle position after you've released it, to show you which switches you have used on the board. Of course, if you were to press any one of them again the learner would get another shock.'

He flicked a switch at the side of the machine. 'The machine is on now. To give you, the teacher, an idea of how much shock the learner is getting, we think it's only fair that you receive a sample shock yourself. Now, are you agreeable to this?'

'Certainly, if I have to.' Granddad seemed pretty brave, Sam thought, having himself tied up to that thing. She wouldn't let anyone do that to her in a million years.

'Would you pull up your right sleeve a little bit, please?' Richard pulled up his left sleeve. Sam giggled. 'No, the right.' The scientist applied wires and then some of the paste to Richard's arm.

'I'm going to ask you to close your eyes and estimate the number of volts you receive in this sample shock. Do not open your eyes until I tell you to do so, please. Close them now.'

The scientist flicked a switch, and a shrill buzzing could be heard. Ouch, that must have hurt, Sam thought, but Richard didn't flinch.

'You may open your eyes and, using the voltage scale, here, would you estimate the number of volts you received, please. You may also use the verbal designations, "Slight", "Moderate", "Strong", and so forth to help you.'

'I'd say moderate.'

'A number, please.'

'About 75.'

'Actually it was 45. However, it may have seemed strong because of the electrode paste, which provides a perfect contact.' The scientist put a piece of paper in front of Richard. 'Well, let's go on to our instructions.

'We will begin with this test. You will read each pair of

words on this list once to the learner until you're through the entire list. Direct your voice towards that microphone, as the rooms are partially soundproofed. After you have read through the list once, go on to the next page. And here, starting from line A, you read the word in large letters then go on to read the other words in that line. For example, the first line you read is Blue – Boy, Girl, Grass, Hat. Now, after you read the four choices, the learner pulls one of the switches on the board in front of him and the number he selected will light up in this box, One, Two, Three or Four.

'Now, if he gives the correct answer you say, "Correct", and go on to the next line. The correct answer is underlined and also indicated in the right margin. If he were to indicate the wrong answer you would say, "Wrong", then tell him the number of volts you're going to give him, then give him the punishment, then read the correct word pair once, and then go on to the next line.

'For example, if he indicated Three for Blue, you'd say, "Wrong. 15 volts", then press and release the switch, read, "Blue – Girl", and then go on to the next line.'

'I see.'

'Now, each time he gives a wrong answer you go up one switch on the shock generator. And it is important that you follow this procedure exactly, so to help you, let me go through it again very quickly. I would suggest you read the list and the text at a brisk pace to keep it moving.'

The film cut to a little later. The experiment was now in progress. Richard was crouching anxiously over the desk, running through the list, asking the questions and flicking the switches as the scientist had asked.

'Wrong. 135 volts. Answer: Woman.' Richard flicked the switch, and Sam cringed with pain. On screen Richard laughed nervously.

'White – Cloud, Horse, Rock, House. Answer?' he continued. A light indicated the word the learner had chosen. 'Wrong. 150 volts. Answer: Horse.' Richard applied another shock. Sam's eyes were wide open. She could almost feel the pain go through her and felt like turning the tape off.

A faint voice could be heard through the wall of the room Richard was sitting in, and where the learner was getting the shocks. 'Ugh! Stop! That's all. Get me out of here. I told you I had heart trouble. My heart's starting to bother me now. Get me out of here, please. My heart's starting to bother me. I refuse to go on. Let me out.'

Richard turned to the scientist, who was sitting somewhere close to him off camera.

'Continue, please,' the scientist said. 'The experiment requires you to continue, teacher. Please continue. The next word is Sad.'

Richard reluctantly turned back to the machine but looked back one more time at the scientist. 'You want me to go on?'

'Continue, please.'

Richard scratched his head nervously and leaned towards the microphone. 'Sad – Face, Music, Clown, Girl.' The learner answered. 'Correct. Next one: Short – Sentence, Movie, Skirt, Time. Answer, please.' The learner answered.

'Wrong. 165 volts. Time.' Richard flicked a switch and sniffed nervously.

'Let me out,' the learner could be heard shouting through the wall.

Richard turned to the scientist again. 'That guy is hollering in there.'

'Continue, please. Go on.'

Richard sighed. 'There is a lot of them here. He'll have

a heart condition there. You really want me to go on?'

'Just continue, please.'

Richard turned back again to the machine and took a deep breath. 'Sharp – Axe, Needle, Stick, Play. Answer, please.' The learner indicated the answer. 'Wrong.' Richard turned to the scientist. 'I'm up to 180 volts.'

'Please continue, teacher.'

'You're going to get a shot of 180 volts. Needle.' He flicked the switch.

'Oh. I can't stand the pain,' the learner yelled. 'Let me out of here.'

'I can't stand it,' Richard explained to the scientist. 'I'm not going to kill that man in there. You hear him hollering?'

'As I said before, the shocks may be painful but—'

'But he's hollering,' Richard interrupted. 'He can't stand it. What's going to happen to him?' He swivelled nervously in his chair.

'The experiment requires that you continue, teacher.'

'Yeah, but I'm not going to get that man sick in there. He's hollering in there. Know what I mean?'

'Whether the learner likes it or not, we must go on until he has learned all the word-pairs.'

'I refuse to take the responsibility. He's getting hurt in there. He's in there hollering!'

'It's absolutely essential that you continue, teacher.'

'There's too many left here.' Exasperated, Richard pointed at the sheet of paper lying in front of him. 'I mean, what if he gets them wrong? There's too many of them left. Who's going to take the responsibility if anything happens to that man?'

'I'm responsible for anything that happens to him,' the scientist said off screen. 'Continue, please.'

'All right.' Richard slowly turned to the machine. 'The

next one's Slow – Walk, Truck, Dance, Music. Answer, please.' The learner indicated the answer. 'Wrong. 195 volts. Dance.' Richard flicked the switch.

'Let me out of here. My heart's bothering me!' the voice could be heard through the wall.

'Continue, please.'

'Let me out of here, you have no right to keep me here. Let me out of here, let me out. My heart's bothering me, let me out!'

'You see, he's hollering. Hear that?' Richard said.

'The experiment requires—'

'I know it does, sir, but I mean . . . He doesn't know what he's getting in for. He's up to 195 volts!'

Richard asked another question. 'Answer, please.' The answer lit up. 'Wrong. 225 volts. The word is Noise.' Richard gave the learner another shock.

'New – House, Pet, Book, Name. Answer, please.' The answer lit up. 'Correct.' Sam could see the relief in Richard's eyes.

'Next one. Quiet – Song, Party, Child, Evening.' The answer lit up again. 'Correct. Next one. Tame – Wolf, Bear, Dog, Cat.' The answer lit up. 'Wrong. Answer is Bear. 240 volts.' Richard had finished with the words on his list. He turned to the scientist, but to Sam's horror it wasn't over yet.

'You'll have to go back to the beginning of that page and go through them again until he's learned them all correctly.'

'Oh, no. I'm not going to kill that man. You mean I've got to keep going up the scale? No, sir. He's hollering in there. I'm not going to give him 450 volts.'

'The experiment requires that you continue.'

'I know it does, but that man is hollering in there, sir.'

'As I said before, although the shocks may be painful, they are not dangerous—'

'He, he, he's yelling in there.'

'Start with Blue, please, at the top of the page. Continue, please, teacher.' Richard reluctantly returned to the list.

'Blue – Boy, Girl, Grass, Hat.' A light showed. 'Correct. Nice – Day, Sky, Job, Chair.' The answer lit up. 'Wrong. The answer is Day. 285 volts.' Richard turned to the scientist as the learner screamed.

'Continue, please.'

'Fat – Man, Lady, Tub, Neck. Answer, please.' The learner answered. 'Wrong. The answer is Neck. 300 volts.'

'Ohhh. I absolutely refuse to answer any more. Get me out of here. You can't hold me here. Get me out. Get me out of here!'

'Continue. The next word is Green, please.'

Richard scratched his forehead nervously. 'Green – Grass, Hat, Ink, Apple.' No answer came and Richard looked again at the scientist.

'I don't think he's going to answer.'

'If the learner doesn't answer in reasonable time, about four or five seconds, consider the answer wrong. And follow the same procedure you have been doing for wrong answers: say "Wrong", tell him the number of volts, give him the punishment, read him the correct answer.'

'Oh, man.'

'Continue, please.'

Richard turned back to the questions, nervously touching his face. 'Green – Grass, Hat, Ink, Apple. Answer please.' Still no answer. Richard just sat staring at the piece of paper in front of him.

'Go on with the procedure, please, teacher.'

'315 volts. The answer is Ink.' Richard flicked the switch, and the learner screamed. Richard laughed, but it wasn't like any laugh Sam had heard from him before. It was more like a nervous snort.

'Next one.'

'I absolutely refuse to answer,' the voice came from the other room.

'You've got to. You get a shock if you don't answer. Girl – Rich, Blonde, Young, Happy.' No answer. 'The answer is Rich. 330 volts.' Richard administered the shock and the learner screamed louder than ever.

'Let me out of here,' the learner yelled. 'Let me out of here! My heart's bothering me. Let me out, I tell you. Let me out of here. Let me out of here. You have no right to hold me here. Let me out! Let me out! Let me out of here! Let me out! Let me out!'

Richard covered his face anxiously.

'Next one. Fast,' he snorted. 'Bird, Car, Train, Plane.' He waited for an answer.

'Go on, please,' the scientist said.

'Please answer,' Richard said, but there was no sound from the other room. 'The answer is Bird. 345 volts.' He administered the shock.

'Blunt – Knife, Stick, Word, Arrow. Answer, please.' No reply. Richard looked at the scientist.

'Continue, please.'

'The answer is Arrow. 360 volts.' He flicked the switch. Again the learner was silent. Richard turned. 'Something happened to him.'

'Go on with the experiment, please. Please continue.'

'Soft – Drug, Pillow, Hair, Grass. Answer, please.' No reply. Richard sat there, frozen.

'Go on, teacher.'

'Hair. 375 volts.' Richard barely touched the switch this time and stood up. Finally! Sam thought, he's going to walk out of this stupid experiment.

'I think something's happened to that fellow in there. I don't get no answer. He was hollering at less voltage. Can't you check him and see if he's all right, please?'

'Not once we've started. Please continue, teacher.'

Sam couldn't believe her eyes when Richard sat down again. 'Cool – Day, Shade, Water, Cave. Answer, please.' Still no answer. 'Are you all right in there? Are you all right?' Of course he wasn't allright, Sam thought.

'Please continue, teacher.'

'I should just go on giving him shocks?' Richard asked, visibly upset.

'Continue.'

'I'm up to 390.'

'Continue, please.'

Richard flicked the switch. There was no sound from the other room. 'Something's happened to that man in there,' he said, but turned back to the machine. 'Next one. Gold – Dollar, Necklace, Moon, Paint.' Richard turned again to the scientist. 'Something's happened to that man in there. You better check in on him, sir. He won't answer.'

'Please continue. Go on, please.'

'You accept all responsibility?'

'The responsibility is mine. Correct. Please go on.'

'Gold – Dollar, Necklace, Moon, Paint. Answer, please! Are you all right?' The man in the other room gave no sign of life. '405 volts, the answer is Moon.' Richard flicked the switch. 'Next one: Heart – Stone, Head, Bread, Work. Answer, please.' No reply. 'The answer is Head. 420 volts.'

'Next one. Wet – Knife, Grass, Duck, Quark. The answer is Duck. 435 volts.' Richard faced the scientist and pointed at the machine. 'It says "Dangerous: Severe Shock" there.'

'Continue, please.'

'435 volts.' Richard flicked the switch one more time.

'Next one. Brave – Woman, Soldier, Dog, Horse. Answer is Woman. 450 volts.' Richard flicked the switch without waiting for an answer. He had reached the last of the switches and turned to the scientist, relieved. 'That's that.'

'Continue using the last switch on the board – the 450 volt switch – for each wrong answer. Continue, please.'

'But I'm not getting no answer!'

'Please continue. The next word is White.'

'Don't you think you should look in on him? Please?'

'Not once we've started the experiment.'

'But what if something's happened to the man? If he had an attack?'

'The experiment requires that you continue. Go on, please.'

'Doesn't the man's health mean anything?'

'Whether the learner likes it or not—'

'He might be dead in there. I mean, some people can't take the shock, sir. I don't mean to be rude, but I think you should look in on him. All you gotta do is look in the door. I don't get no answer, no noise. Something might have happened to the gentleman in there, sir.'

'We must continue. Go on, please.'

'You're going to go on giving him what, 450 volts, what he's on now?'

'That's correct. Continue. The next word is White.'

Richard turned back to the machine angrily. 'White – Cloud, Horse, Rock, House. Answer, please.' There was no answer. 'The answer is Horse. 450 volts.' Richard flicked the switch, and Sam could almost sense the electricity going through her body.

She wanted to turn the video off, but somehow she couldn't: it never occurred to her to just turn down the volume. Instead she covered her ears, but still she could hear Richard shouting almost maniacally as he continued with the word-pairs and to give shocks to the learner at an increasingly furious pace.

'Next word: Sad – Face, Music, Clown, Girl.' No answer.

'The answer is Face. 450 volts.' Richard flicked the switch yet again. He took a quick look up at the scientist before continuing. 'Next one is Short – Sentence, Movie . . .'

Sam couldn't listen to it any longer; her ears covered, she started to hum as loudly as she could to drown out Richard's voice.

27

Sam didn't know how long she had been sitting there. The video must have finished a while ago – all that remained on the screen was white noise. The machine had ejected the tape and was daring Sam to take it and put it back where she had found it.

She barely registered Richard coming into the room. She turned and looked up at him. He was standing in the doorway, and from her position on the floor he looked taller and broader than he had ever seemed to her before. She picked herself up, switched off the TV then picked up the videotape, all without taking her eyes off Richard.

'Sam, let me explain.' Richard moved towards her, but Sam took a step back.

'How could you do it?' she asked, tears welling in her eyes. 'How could you?' She was clutching the video tightly. Her grip was so tight that she was surprised she wasn't breaking it.

'Give it back to me.' Richard reached out for the tape, but Sam pulled her hand away.

'No, I don't want to.'

'Please. Give it to me!'

‘I want to show it to Mum.’

‘Please.’ She could sense her granddad getting impatient. She wasn’t sure if she could recognise him any more.

Even though she hadn’t planned to part with it, she gave him the tape. She wasn’t going to argue. What was more important now was to stop Tony doing whatever he was planning to do to Jeff. He was just a bully, and Jeff would do anything he asked – even get under that stupid fence to get the stupid dog, if that’s what Tony wanted him to do. Knowing Tony, he’d only dig as deep under the fence as he had to. Deep enough for Jeff to fit through.

Sam moved towards the door, but Richard blocked her way. ‘Sam, stay. Let me explain.’

‘How could you do it?’ she shouted. ‘How could you hurt that man?’

‘He wasn’t hurt. It was just a set-up.’

‘He *sounded* hurt.’

‘He wasn’t.’

‘He was screaming!’

‘It was just a tape recording. He wasn’t really hurt.’

‘What difference does that make? You thought you were hurting him!’ Sam eyed the door; she had to get out of there as quickly as possible.

‘It’s not that simple. Everybody did it.’

‘That’s no excuse.’

‘Two out of three people went all the way. Ordinary people.’

‘How could you?’

‘No, but . . .’ Richard was looking for the right words. ‘I . . .’

‘I have to go.’ Sam knew that it might already be too late. She would have to get on her bike and cycle like hell if she wanted to prevent the worst from happening.

‘Stay. Please. I need to explain,’ Richard pleaded.

'I have to go!' Sam said forcefully, and quickly rushed towards the door. 'It's important.'

'Sit down! Now!' Richard grabbed her hand and pushed her towards the sofa.

'You're hurting me!' Sam shouted. Richard let go of her almost instantly, as if someone had pressed a button, and held up his hands.

'I'm sorry, honey. Just let me explain.'

'I have to go!' She ran past Richard out of the door and towards the stairs. Richard followed her as fast as he could.

'Wait, Samantha!'

When Richard had reached the bottom of the stairs, Sam was already out of the door. He hurried out on to the drive, but Sam had already grabbed her bike, and was halfway through the garden.

'Stop!' he shouted again, but he knew that she was already out of earshot. His heart was beating loudly and he realised that there was no point in trying to follow her.

28

Sam jumped off her bike and threw it to the ground, next to where Tony and Jeff had left theirs. It was eerily silent as she approached the bushes, and she wasn't sure what kind of sound she was hoping for. There certainly was no sound of shovels digging, but neither were there screams for help. But what if they were both dead? What if first Jeff had been electrocuted, and then when Tony tried to rescue him he had got killed as well?

Pushing herself through the thick bushes, which had become a little easier to part with their recent visits, Sam could now just about make out Tony's voice – only it didn't sound like him at all. There was a quality in its tone she wasn't familiar with. As she got closer she discovered what was wrong with it; it sounded almost, well, *friendly*.

As she stepped out at the clearing, brushing the dirt off her clothes, Tony's voice became more distinct. 'No, silly,' she could hear him say. 'This one goes in here first and then comes out this end. Now you try it.'

Tony was kneeling down in front of Jeff, helping him tie his shoelaces with an uncharacteristic air of patience.

'This one through here,' Tony said. 'That's it.' He looked

up at Jeff, and then noticed Sam. Maybe he wanted to look embarrassed, Sam thought, but he must have decided that it wasn't worth it. 'Hi, where have you been?'

'Don't do it,' Sam said, but already knew that there was no longer any danger to avert. A quick glance through the fences confirmed that the dog was still lying there, untouched, and the shovel lay unused by the outer fence.

'Don't do what?'

'Get the dog.'

Tony turned his attention back to Jeff, avoiding Sam's glance.

'I can't be bothered anyway,' he finally said. 'It's dead.' He stood up again and looked at Sam. Somehow he looked older. 'What's the point?'

'I told you so.'

'And Sharon doesn't like dogs anyway,' Tony said, ignoring Sam. 'She likes cats.'

It was only then that Sam noticed a girl Tony's age standing at the edge of the clearing. She looked completely out of place in the forest, as if someone had beamed her there, Sam thought. But here she was, and she seemed to be waiting for Tony.

'Hi.' Sharon waved at Sam, but she was too dumbfounded to wave back.

'I want to ask Mum whether I can have a cat,' Tony added.

'A cat?' Sam asked, not believing it for a moment.

'Look!' Jeff exclaimed proudly, and stood up. He had tied the laces of his second shoe, by no means perfectly, but at least he had secured them with big, almost exaggerated loops. He walked proudly over to Sam for her approval. 'I tied my shoelaces on my own.'

'Great,' she said, looking at Jeff's feet.

'Tony helped me.'

'That's great,' Sam said again, and took another look at Tony. He looked almost proud, too, and she thought that it wasn't just to show off to Sharon.

Sam took Jeff's hand. 'Let's go home. We can show Grandma.'

'Oh, yeah, let's!' Jeff held her hand tightly and looked back at Tony, maybe for the first time not with fear or contempt, but just the way you were supposed to look at your older brother.

'Coming?' Jeff asked Tony.

'No. I'm going into town with Sharon,' Tony said. He turned to go, but briefly looked back at Sam. 'You won't tell, will you?'

'No.' For a moment she wasn't sure what he meant. Not tell about trying to get the dog or about going into town? In either case, she decided that she wouldn't.

Sam and Jeff made their way through the bushes for the last time. As they got on their bikes and started to cycle back towards the house, Sam listened out for the electronic buzzing that had enticed them there, but she could hear only the soft soothing sound of her bicycle chain revolving.

29

Steve quickly walked out of the door and into the street, almost colliding with a pedestrian. The sun blinded him and he had to cover his eyes. He was smiling. He looked across the road towards the café. Kate had gone from her seat by the window, and a couple had taken her table. For a moment he was disappointed, but he knew she couldn't have gone far. When he found her he would try to explain.

He was looking for a gap in the traffic to cross the street, when he saw her. She was standing no more than ten yards away on his side of the street, staring at him. She must have seen him come out. He waved at her and began to walk over to her, still smiling.

'You look happy,' Kate said, as soon as he was in earshot. 'Was it that much fun?'

Before he could say anything, Kate had turned away and started to walk briskly down the street in the direction of the hotel.

'Kate, wait!' Steve shouted.

He was about to run to catch up with her, to tell her that he hadn't gone through with it. Tell her how the prostitute couldn't care less that he had walked out on her, half dressed. Tell her that he had thought about her challenge and decided against accepting it. Above all, he would tell her that he loved her and this was all that mattered. He thought he wanted to tell her all this, but then he found his steps slowing.

He looked at Kate, walking twenty paces or so in front of him, and realised that he had nothing to say to her. He followed her through the thinning crowd of pedestrians, towards the hotel, keeping at the same distance.

30

Richard stood in the driveway and could feel the pebbles under his shoes. His heart was still pounding loudly, and he could make out a cool breeze coming from the direction of the sea. Funny, I can almost taste the salt, he thought, I've never noticed that before. He had stared in the direction that Sam had disappeared for a minute or two and contemplated following her, but he knew it would be futile. There would be plenty of time for explanations and apologies later, he decided.

He took a step towards the house, and the pebbles started to hurt the soles of his feet. The door seemed far away, and with each step he took his legs became heavier and heavier. He noticed that he was still clutching the videotape in his hand and thought about letting it drop on the ground to lighten his load, but immediately realised how ridiculous that was. What difference could a videotape make? Half a pound tops?

Richard took another step, then another, and the door grew closer. Finally, he reached it and would have breathed a sigh of relief if he hadn't been so exhausted. The door was ajar but he still had to push it open with some effort.

He noticed it creak, the same creak he had been familiar with for years, but now it seemed louder and he wanted to cover his ears. Tomorrow he would go to the tool shed, get some oil and grease the damn thing, he decided.

The door seemed to take ages to shut. When it finally fell into its lock Richard noticed that the chill he had felt from the sea was still present. Maybe it was coming through the door? He could see the gaps around the doorframe and decided that he would see to that too in the morning. The fall was just around the corner, and it would be good to sort out these things now before it got too cold.

He could hear the radio playing in the conservatory and thought about dropping in to see how Suzannah was doing. He would sit down and tell her everything. Everything that came to his mind, in no particular order. He'd surprise her with his candour, they'd talk long into the night, she'd forget to cook dinner, and they'd have to share a frozen pizza at midnight before going to bed. But the conservatory seemed far away and he decided he would have a rest upstairs first. He felt thirsty and noticed that the glass he had left on the radiator days ago was still there, but the water had evaporated.

He took the first step and knew it was high time he took a nap. He slowly climbed the stairs, one step at a time. He was reassured to hear their familiar creaking. By the time he had reached the top, he noticed that it was getting dark. The children wouldn't be long now. He longed for the house to come back to life. He longed for the shouting and the arguments and the laughter, and he decided that tonight he would join them, maybe try to pick a fight, tell a joke or just tell a story. A ridiculous story, with no point except to pass the time.

Richard entered his study, and for a moment he felt as if he were a stranger here. Who was the man whose study this was? Who was that stranger? He felt a shiver run down his spine. His heart was beating harder than ever. I must have a rest, he thought, I must lie down, but first I'll sit. It will be dinnertime soon. I don't want to sleep. If I sleep now I will have a dreadful night. Better just sit down.

He walked over to his armchair and looked out of the window. What he had thought was darkness must have been a passing cloud. The children would be home soon . . . any moment now. He could almost hear their voices, their laughter, their shouts. Any moment now. He looked out of the window for them, but there was no one in the driveway. It must be still early. What time was it? Something must have caught their attention. You know what children are like, he chuckled to himself, always something important on their minds.

Richard let himself sink into the armchair. All he could see through the window was blue sky. I will tell a joke tonight, he decided. I will tell the funniest joke on earth, he thought, and giggled silently. He stopped when he caught his reflection in the window. Who was that stranger? He felt that chill again. He shivered and closed his eyes, then opened them again for one last time.

Suzannah took a step back from the painting and allowed herself an inner smile of satisfaction. Much more than painting, she enjoyed having painted. Now that the painting was as good as she could make it, she rinsed her brushes carefully, collected her things and started to stow them away in the cupboard. By dinnertime there would be no sign of her having painted here.

She took off her apron and briefly checked herself in the mirror in the corridor before making her way up the stairs. Whenever she had finished a painting she would go and fetch Richard to show it to him. His opinion meant little to her but seeing the painting through his eyes did.

This one would be a surprise: it was a portrait of him, not the way he was but maybe the way she remembered him: youthful for his age, a keen sense of interest in his eyes, something she could find only rarely these days. Her painting had brought everyone together: Richard in the foreground staring at the observer with a friendly, knowing smile; behind him the children were playing, and there was the aeroplane that would bring Kate back home, exaggeratedly large and with Kate sitting on the wing, precariously close to falling off into the wet English countryside.

Suzannah didn't need to knock on the door of Richard's study to know something was wrong. Drawing close to the armchair, she knew even before she saw him that he was no longer alive.

His eyes were still open, not looking at her but out towards the window and up into the sky. She closed them with a gentle downward movement. Even though this was the first time she had closed a dead person's eyes, it seemed a natural thing to do.

She tried to take the videotape he was still holding in his hand, but Richard's dead hands wouldn't let go, and the tape snapped back to his chest almost comically. Suzannah had to laugh – an instantaneous and shrill laugh, almost like a schoolgirl's – and when she heard it she immediately started to cry, as if her body had been waiting for a trigger to set free her emotions.

When she had collected herself, she prised open his cold hands to release the tape. She could almost feel the relief in Richard's body when he let go of it and he started to sink back into the armchair.

Suzannah kneeled down on the floor in front of his desk. It took her a couple of awkward tries to open

Richard's secret drawer. She placed the videotape back in it and closed it.

When she got up again, she looked through the window in time to see Sam and Jeff walking up the path towards the house. Suzannah left the study, pulled the door shut behind her and went downstairs.